MW01613674

Through the

Woods

Lauren Redding

Table of Contents

Dedicated to the people who believe in me, inspire me, and push me to be the best version of myself. And to God who saw me through it all and guided me here.

Copyright © 2018 by Lauren Redding

All rights reserved. No part of this book may be reproduced or used in any manner without written permission of the copyright owner except for the use of quotations in a book review. For more information, address: laurenredding1410@gmail.com

FIRST EDITION

Laurenredding.weebly.com

Pronunciation Guide:

Aoife (Ee+fa)

Neasa (Nyas+a)

Ailbe (All+bay)

Caoihme (Kee+va)

Cahal (Kal)

Eamonn (Aim+an)

Saibhreas (Said+bres)

Laoch (Lay+uk)

Prologue

Into the woods they would walk, laughing and exploring all the paths that lay hidden behind the curtain of branches. Aoife had not a care in the world. Why would she? Her parents loved her, and they would spend hours together having adventures that laid beyond the walls of her home. Her mother was the one to always suggest venturing, dragging her father and Aoife along. When the little family would wander into the village and nothing seemed to divide her family from those of the villagers. Nothing but a crown distinguished her father from another man. After long days spent among the people, the little family would read by the fire; Aoife would sit at the feet of her mother, listening to the soft hums of her parents' voices as it lulled her to sleep. Aoife considered herself to be the happiest person in the world.

Until she wasn't. That was the day her mother went into the forest alone and never returned--attacked by mercenaries pretending to be beggars, that is what her father told her. Aoife watched her father weep for days. She thought he would break, he became hard instead, shutting himself away from Aoife. All the warmth that had filled her days ended, like the warmth of day giving way to the bitterness of night.

Aoife learned to paint a smile on her face, masking her own pain. She would retreat into the woods to hide from the grief that would drown her, where she could feel close to her mother. It became Aoife's secret, her father forbid her to go alone into the woods, for, he warned,

"Stay on the path, girl, never stray. There are wolves who wear the faces of men."

What big eyes you have.

The better to *see* you with, my dear.

Chapter One

Aoife awoke with a start; books were scattered across her bed, weighing down the sheets. Aoife shifted them gently to escape from her bed.

A crisp breeze rustled through the trees, creating a soft rush of music. As far as she could look, a sea of trees surrounded the castle, creating a barrier between the castle and the forest. The leaves were starting to explode with colors: red, gold and orange smothered the green. Just beyond the borders of the woods, Aoife saw the wisp of smoke that rose from the village; people were waking with the dawn.

A small smile grew on Aoife's face. Autumn was in the air; the crops soon would be cut down and harvested and stored away for the village to prepare for the harsh uncertainty of winter. Every harvest, after the last crop was in, a festival was held in celebration for the abundance that was found in the Kingdom of Saibhreas. Everyone gathered from the kingdom to join in the merriment. For three days the market center was crowded with people. A huge fire burned at the center of the town to light the path, women shared stories, while the men drank ale. The young maidens would dance to the beat of the drums the young men would watch their eyes hungry with wonder, like animals.

For years, King Eamonn only let Aoife join the last night of the festival when he would go, and he could watch her. This year, however, he promised she could attend the whole of it, from every merchant's booth to the dancing. Excitement spread through her body, wished time would go by faster.

Aoife's walls were filled with shelves stuffed with books. Her room was large, allowing for a bed and a couple of dressers. Her room held the coolness of the morning, small embers burned in the fire fading slowly into nothing. It was odd to see the fire that low, *where was Neasa*? The old woman was normally here before Aoife awoke. *Perhaps she slept late. No matter,* she laughed to herself.

Aoife dressed in a simple blue frock. Walking over to her mirror, she examined herself closely. Her pale, golden hair fell to her waist in waves. Her eyes were like cornflowers with gray circling the blue. She had a soft complexion with lips the color of raspberries; almost as if she had eaten too many as a child and they had eternally stained her lips. She combed her fingers through her hair and braided it to keep from covering her face.

She was about to gather her books when a knock came to the door. Before she could answer, her father barged into her space. His cold gaze searched the room, analyzing everything he could see. Aoife stiffened at the judgement that rolled off her father.

"Glad to see you are taking your studies seriously." His voice was clipped.

Aoife's face colored a deep shade of pink at his tone. A small smile formed automatically on her mouth, a learned response from years of hiding her real feelings from King Eamonn. She didn't have the courage to tell the king that these books were simply for enjoyment. The books Rowan had given her were placed neatly in a pile on the dresser by her bed. Her father didn't seem to notice that the books scattered across her bed were her mother's. Aoife came toward him to divert his gaze. If he continued to observe, it would not take him long to place where she had gotten the books.

She missed his smile. King Eamonn was a tall man with eyes the color of iron that gleamed like a blade under light. His soft brown hair was fading into gray, just like autumn fades into winter, taking all color and life with its ice.

"Uhm, yes, well, I must be off to go fetch Maeve before studies." She turned away from her father, gathering her books from the bedside table.

"Maeve still joins you?" he said rather absently, no longer looking toward his daughter, but rather into the air as if he were seeing something Aoife could not. "Well, I will make this brief. We will be having a few guards from the Laoch Kingdom coming to stay with us until the festival of harvest. Their main reasons for coming are to train my men to fight better and the second is to keep an eye on you." His tone had a strange finality to it.

Confusion swept through Aoife.

She slowly turned back towards her father, keeping the same smile in place as to not give emotions away. Her heart raced as she asked, "Why would they need to look after me?"

Aoife watched as King Eamonn's shoulders sunk lower in place as if she had placed another weight upon them. He rubbed his face with the palm of his hand.

"My daughter, it is not easy to be a king. Hard decisions must be made for the protection of our people. Even if the cost is our own happiness. Do you understand?"

She nodded slowly comprehending the words, but not understanding what any of this had to do with the warriors who were to be their guests.

He continued. "I have tried to protect you, but Saibhreas has many enemies struggling to gain the abundance of our people." He paused, the king consumed the father. "Daughter, our enemies are forming against us, and I must do what's best for the safety of our people."

This was the first time that King Eamonn had spoken with Aoife about the kingdom. She realized now, much as she had when she was a child, that her world was not as perfect as it seemed to her. Her father had protected her from the truth and she was not sure whether she should thank him, or scream. Perhaps her father was just being paranoid, like he was about the woods. She wanted to believe that nothing could hurt them further.

"Father, what is best?"

Her father's eyebrows raised in surprise, a faint look of relief lit his face.

"I have told King Kieran that you would marry his son when you turn eighteen. In exchange, our men will be trained in combat with the best warriors. We will have security. And you will have a husband and someone to rule our land with."

"But all seems well. What dangers are you speaking of, father?"

He looked away, he didn't look her in the eye.

"There is always conflict when land is involved…" His voice trailed off.

Aoife didn't know if he truly had gotten lost in his thoughts or if he had told her everything he wanted to say. She could never fully understand him, not like her mother could.

She had never really considered marriage until that moment. In three months, she was to be sold off like cattle to a prince to be a barter price for the land of Laoch. The Laoch kingdom was the biggest and fiercest in all the land. Aoife had heard the tales of their animal-like ferocity in battle; they conquered. Saibhreas was still its own because of a deal King Eamonn had made with King Kieran, but it seemed they, too, would be swallowed up by the warriors of Laoch.

She understood what her father meant about sacrifices for the good of the people—they would lose themselves to save the people—but why did she have to be the one to be sold? Couldn't they pay Laoch with coin instead of her life? Did her father want to be rid of her that badly? Was she really such a burden?

"Will this make you happy, Father?" she asked. His brow pinched together again in surprise. If he spent more time with her, if he would really find her acceptance so unnerving. She wanted her father to be happy again.

Besides, she thought, *my future husband will be gone conquering more land for the kingdom.* She smiled slightly at her own thoughts, if she was lucky she would see her husband as often as she saw her father. The King eyed her warily.

He finally looked her in the eyes, but he remained silent, as if the question had evaporated before them both.

Her heart fell in disappointment. "I better go to Maeve now, Father. Was that all?"

"Stay close to the castle. Dangers lurk in the shadows of the woods." He turned on his heel and left the room without looking back.

Aoife looked out her window once more. Saibhreas castle was settled on top of a hill surrounded by forest. Past the trees, it was about an hour walk from the castle to the village. Her eyes filled with tears, she blinked them away. An automatic smirk concealed the uncertainty she felt inside.

Chapter 2

Aoife finally reached the halfway point. Sneaking out of the gates had always been easy for Aoife, the guards were never strict while on watch duty. If the king ever knew that she left the castle grounds she would be locked in her room…until her wedding. Aoife's stomach churned again at the thought of being given away so freely. She knew no more of Laoch then the tales' travelers who visited the village spun for anyone who would hear, and stories were always half-truths anyway.

Maeve was perched in a tree reading when Aoife finally arrived. Maeve was Aoife's dearest friend. Her wide eyes were the color of the earth, Maeve stood a head shorter than Aoife. She had chestnut hair that fell straight down her back, landing at her waist.

Maeve was delicate in features; elegance radiated from her effortlessly. Maeve could turn any man's head by simply walking past them. Maeve was a slight woman with lean muscle, though that was to be credited to her work on her father's farm. Aoife used to help Maeve and her family in the fields until the King found out and forbade her from laboring with the family.

Aoife grinned and waved to her friend perched in the tree.

"One of these days, I'm going to find you turned into a bird. And you will fly far away and see many great things." She laughed.

Maeve's smile lit up her face. "Aye, that's an idea. I could go far away. I could go anywhere! Think of the adventures I would find myself in."

Aoife shook her head. "You really are too restless for this small corner of the world. When you learn to fly, just remember to land here for the winters."

Maeve clamored down the tree with the ease of a woodland animal. She stood across her friend dusting off dirt from her the skirt of her dress.

"I would come back. My family is here." She placed her hands on her hips looking at her friend with a cocked head as if she could sense something was off.

Aoife clicked her tongue to try to distract Maeve. Knowing the second she told Maeve the reality of her life would settle in around her.

"And I am here."

Maeve stepped forward and linked arms with Aoife. Aoife's heart swelled with the love in the gesture. Maeve looked into her eyes, all seriousness. "Family is more than blood." She smiled carefully at Aoife and moved them in the direction of the castle. "You are my family too."

Aoife squeezed her arm in response, afraid that if she opened her mouth, all that would come would be tears. Aoife could not be sure of her father anymore. Her parents used to be one soul occupying two bodies. When she lost her mother, all those years ago, the father she knew and loved left her as well. All that remained was the shell of King Eamonn.

Maeve and Aoife walked in a comfortable silence.

When Aoife still had both her parents with they wanted the love of the people and to love them in return. They had always told her that serving the people helped to remind a ruler that one was not better than the people they served. Aoife's mother used to tell her that a stiff neck made a crown heavy. They would go throughout the week to the village and interact with the people. The king would till the ground with the men, her mother would socialize with the other women, leaving Aoife to play with the other children in the village. Maeve had come over to Aoife and pulled her from her mother's skirts dragging her to play with the other girls. From then on Maeve and Aoife were inseparable. And though that hadn't changed, the king had, he rarely visited the village and his daughter was never supposed to leave the castle.

After Aoife lost her mother, Maeve stepped in to comfort her in her grief. King Eamonn had seen that Maeve was useful to his daughter and allowed Maeve to join Aoife in her studies, hoping that would appease his daughter long enough for the Rowan to teach her. What no one but Aoife had foreseen was that Maeve would excel in the studies, becoming useful to the kingdom thereby secreting her spot in Aoife's life for always.

"The king came to see me this morning." Aoife sighed.

Maeve squeezed her friend's arm. "Whatever for?" Curiosity clung to every word. Aoife told Maeve of the events that had unfolded earlier that morning. Maeve watched Aoife carefully, her deep eyes searching her friends.

"There has to be another solution," Maeve said.

"My father insisted he would do it no other way. I—I just hope the prince is kind."

"I am sure he will be. If he was not, your father would not arrange a marriage."

Aoife was uncertain of that, but she kept that thought to herself. "What do you think he is like?" Aoife asked, hoping that the desperation she felt didn't reflect with the tone of her voice.

A bright smile formed around Maeve's mouth and patting the princess's arm said, "He will be kind."

Maeve chatted with Aoife distracting her thoughts all the way back to the castle.

***

"So, you did decide to come," Rowan growled "Tardiness is unbecoming of a lady." He said, looking pointedly at Aoife.

Rowan was tall and round. His face was always the color of a tomato, which sadly matched his hair perfectly, making his face just one lump of red. Completing the image, his green eyes seemed to always be bulging out of his head.

Today, however, Aoife was not in the mood to deal with grumpy old men. *There were far too many in the castle,* she thought. Starting with the king. She mumbled an apology as she and Maeve took their seats. Throughout the lesson, Aoife couldn't concentrate. What had she learned of the Laoch kingdom? She racked her brain as Rowan's voice filled the background of her thoughts with a dull roar. They had the greatest army that is what her father had said. What did that mean of the prince? Would he be cruel? Would he fill Saibhreas with his wars? Would he listen to her?

As Rowan's gravel voice filled her ears, a dread settled itself in her stomach.

Chapter 3

The week went by in a blur, and Aoife's anxiety grew with each day that passed. Aoife wore a cheery mask as her news spread through the kingdom. Walking down the halls of the castle, Aoife could hear her name being whispered amid excited giggles from every servant she passed. The men in the palace looked either pleased or disappointed. *Well at least there is that to be grateful for, no more men trying to gain her hand for marriage, she was already claimed.*

The King had kept his distance from his daughter, causing Aoife anxiety. *Was he not pleased? What more did he want?* The men from Laoch were expected to arrive at any time, and Aoife felt as if an invisible chain had enclosed itself around her neck like a serpent, tightening with each day that passed.

Aoife couldn't stand to be in the confines of the castle with the growing anxiety building inside her chest. She left with Maeve and took to exploring the deeper part of the woods. Aoife knew she was hiding from her responsibilities, and her stomach seemed to weave itself into a knot as Maeve chattered about some plant and when the sound of her voice slipped into silence. Aoife raised her head toward Maeve to see what caused the abrupt end to her words. Maeve stared at her, hands on her hips.

"Aoife I can see that you are not yourself." Maeve's deep brown eyes softened. "I can see that your smile is for the sake of others. You will be run over by those men if you don't stop now. You may not have much of a choice in who you marry, but you always have a choice in your reaction."

Maeve was, as usual, correct. Only Aoife could allow someone else to exercise power over her; it was her choice to act or to let life dictate her happiness. Aoife's mouth twitched in bitter humor.

Maeve continued, "Besides, sorrow is not good for the complexion. Wouldn't want your prince to receive word that his bride-to-be has the wrinkles of an old woman already." She laughed.

Her prince? A fluttering started in her stomach. She rubbed her hands across her face. Aoife could tell Maeve was holding back further comments as she shook her head. "I understand what you mean, Maeve. I will listen to your counsel."

Maeve took a minute to respond. Aoife could tell Maeve was weighing her words to see if Aoife was sincere. She must have found her answer, she exclaimed "Good! You are much more enjoyable being true to yourself." She winked.

Aoife decided to push the thoughts from her mind and let her spirit ease. They continued to chatter on until the brightness of the day bled into dusk.

"I must head home. Mother will worry." Maeve sighed and nudged Aoife with her shoulder. "Aoife, you— I will see you tomorrow."

"Be safe, Maeve." Aoife smiled and this time it was genuine.

Dusk faded into night, the moon was full in the sky and the white light of it lit Aoife's path under her feet. Aoife was sure she could find her way home even in the dark. She knew every twist and turn that lay before her on the road. She hummed a lullaby and grabbed at the passing branches.

As she looked up, a silhouette appeared before her on the pathway. Aoife cursed herself for not seeing it earlier. She moved into the oblivion that the trees provided. The shape moved closer, seeming not to have seen her. The man's body was tight with muscles as he approached. The rest of his features were mixed in with the night. She drew further back. As the figure drew closer, something on his chest glinted in the moon's light.

She squinted, the symbol looked familiar to her, but she couldn't remember where she had seen it before, it looked like a beast of some kind, but she couldn't make out the shape.

She cursed herself again for not taking more heed to the king's words about staying close to home, her breath caught in her throat.

She sucked in her breath…Laoch. The ensign of Laoch was a wolf, it was a symbol of how the warriors of Laoch fought. She drew back further into the shadows. A twig snapped, and she heard it like thunder during a storm. She flinched and hoped the man didn't hear noise. When she looked back to the path, the man was gone. Her heart galloped in her chest. He had left? The hair stood on the back of her neck. Lowering herself to the ground, she searched the forest floor for a weapon. She came upon a rock the size of her fist and grabbed it.

She hesitated a second longer before she moved to the path once again. A shadow fell across her face and she turned. The figure was in front of her. She saw the flash of a sword and her body went rigid. Remembering her mother, she was ready to slam the stone into the head of the man in front of her. A warm, calloused hand wrapped around her wrist, cutting off her attack.

"Wouldn't it have been better to run?" the man asked, his face concealed in shadows.

"Have you ever tried to run in a dress? I had better chances of survival by fighting," she retorted. She stood taller, hoping he didn't see her body trembling in fear.

He sheathed his sword and released Aoife's hand, watching her closely as he stepped back. He stood a head taller than her and had a stocky build, making Aoife feel like a doll in comparison.

"It is a calm night for a walk in the woods, though calm and safe do not always mean the same thing. What are you doing here so late at night?" She saw his lips curving into a small smile.

"I had some business with the trees, it's a secret though, so I must be—"

He laughed, the sound set Aoife's face a flame. It was so youthful, it surprised her to come from such a gruff man.

"And what are you doing here besides prying into strangers' business?" She demanded, wanting to turn the questions back to him.

The youthful joy vanished. "I was exploring. I heard there was a great treasure in this land, enough, it is said, to make a man rich, and I mean to find it."

Was this what the king meant this morning? Aoife didn't know what to say to that, so she nodded and tried to move around him, but he moved with her, blocking her path. Anger and fear rose in her throat like bile.

"May I walk you back? It is dangerous for a young woman to wander in the woods by herself at night, business with the trees or not. Where are you headed?"

His eyes reflected in the night's light, Aoife had never seen eyes that color before, she shivered and took a step back to retreat from the man. Knowing that one could never trust a stranger they met in the woods.

"I can manage getting home." She took another step away from him.

He bowed. "My name is Liam." His tone was light, but Aoife thought that he was being entirely serious.

She stared at him not knowing if she should laugh or run.

"May I have your name?" He stretched out his hand.

She folded her arms. "Aoife."

The hairs stood back on her neck. "Good luck finding the...eh...treasure."

She hurried away from him, distancing herself from the stranger in the woods. Before she was too far away she thought she heard the stranger whisper reverently, "I think I just found it."

Chapter 4

Aoife paced around her room, the next morning, waiting for Neasa to arrive. The encounter Aoife had last night meant that her guards had arrived to safeguard her until the prince came to claim her himself. Aoife didn't know if she should be flattered or disgusted that the prince would go to such lengths to protect his prize. She groaned inwardly, she hardly needed protection. Though her father claimed there were enemies, Aoife couldn't be sure that he wasn't just being overprotective.

A knock pounded at the door before it creaked open, chasing all thoughts Aoife had away into the morning light. Neasa entered the room with bundles of fabrics in all shades of colors in her hands. She laid them out on the bed, ignoring the fact that Aoife was still under the covers.

"Good morning, Princess. I trust that you slept well."

Aoife smiled at her nurse. Neasa was a round woman with rough hands from years of work. She had a motherly nature, though Aoife knew she had no children of her own.

When Aoife was younger, she used to ask Neasa if she wanted children. Until one day the warm, round lady finally scoffed and said, "I have no time for my own children. You are good enough for me."

There was truth to her words, Neasa had become Aoife's guardian after her mother had died. King Eamonn had wanted his daughter to still have a motherly influence in her life. Aoife loved Neasa and was grateful to the woman for loving her in return, but sometimes Aoife would wonder if he just couldn't face raising his daughter alone.

"Dear Neasa, what is this?" She waved her hands at all the colors on her bed. Neasa was running around the room gleaning the books that were scattered on the room. She had a very concentrated look on her face as though she was trying to think of anything else but Aoife's question.

Aoife left the comfort of her bed and sidled closer to her maid. "Neasa?"

Aoife couldn't question Neasa further because serving girls started to come in, and Neasa ordered them about. They moved about her room in a flurry, as if their skirts were caught on fire. The king must have something planned for her. She retreated to the window, watching the men and women going in and out of the castle walls. It seemed that with the visit of the Laoch warriors brought more chaos to the palace.

Aoife smiled and turned toward the nearest maid, Aideen. Aoife asked the girl what was being done in the village to prepare for the festival. The girl blushed, perhaps being surprised that Aoife knew her name. Not too long the other girls were joining in, the room filled with voices and giggles.

One of the girls directed Aoife to the bath, and afterward, Aoife was dressed by the flurry of women. As Neasa finally came to stand in front of Aoife, excitement oozed from the woman.

"Princess, last night warriors from Laoch arrived at the castle. You father has been with them in his study and will continue to do so for the rest of the afternoon. He has ordered that you stay here with me today. We have much work to do before the festival to prepare you."

Aoife tried to cut her off, but Neasa put her hands up to silence the princess. "The king has ordered this. I am sorry, Princess. Tonight, you are to join the men for a feast to welcome our guests. Your father wants you there." Her aged face shone with eagerness.

Aoife's jaw clenched as she smiled up at her maid, nodding her consent. Really all Aoife did though was comply with the decision that had already been made for her.

"Aideen, what will you wear for the festival?"

The girl looked down. "I suppose this, Princess."

"Do you not have anything else to wear?"

The girl flushed and shook her head. She looked around at the girls around her wondering if it was still possible to have poverty in the wealthiest kingdom in the land. She flushed at her ignorance; Rowan would have her head if he ever knew. If she couldn't change the world today, maybe there was something else she could do. Her thoughts got lost in the noise of the room as she stood on a chair and was poked and prodded. All different colors of fabric were thrust into her face to find the ones most suitable to compliment her complexion and flaxen hair.

She knew it was not Neasa's fault. The king had ordered her imprisonment for the day. Well, if the king wanted a docile princess, then that was exactly what he would get. For now.

***

Neasa had left her with an hour to herself. Needing fresh air, feeling suffocated by the walls around her, Aoife had snuck to the entrance of woods, so that she could be seen from the castle gates, Aoife wanted to read to take her mind from its worry, when the warmth of the sun had curled about her, lulling her into sleep. She had awoken when she heard Neasa calling her name.

The king was going to be furious. She could almost feel his anger emanating from the walls as she walked quickly. As she approached the door to the banquet hall, she raised her chin and forced a smile. She hoped she didn't look as flustered as she felt. As she entered the hall, the noise of grumbling men came to a halt. Chairs screeched as the men stood while Aoife approached the king. When she reached her seat next to the king's he leaned toward her.

"You're late." He snapped in her ear.

She bowed deeply, not meeting her father's sharp gaze. "Yes, my king. I...eh—lost track of time."

He waved her forward and as she sat next to him, he whispered, "Your nose stuck in a book is not more important than our guests." His tone was always unforgiving.

Her face flamed as she tried to keep the smile plastered on her face. "Forgive me, my king." She bit her tongue as to not say more and upset *her king* further. He grunted at her and stood to address the other men in the room. Aoife noted that she was the only woman in the room and wondered if they thought it was odd that she had joined the party.

"Friends, take your seats." A loud scraping filled the room as the men sat down and resumed their meals in front of them. Nerves made Aoife's stomach churn; the food placed in front of her was wasted as she avoided her meal. The king waited as the voices fell way into sounds of hungry men chewing.

"We welcome our guests. They rode a long way to join us at our table." The men grunted like pigs at a trough. "As you all are aware, the surrounding tribes are beginning to grow restless. They want our land. They come closer to our borders every day, killing and plundering anything and everyone in their path."

The kingdom's generals stood, profanity spilling from their lips like drool from a hound. Aoife's brow furrowed in confusion, why was this the first time Aoife had heard this? Until this moment she hadn't understood why they needed Loach's protection. Maybe the king didn't want to get rid of her, it really was for her people.

She remembered that morning he had informed her of her engagement. Perhaps the king wanted her to understand the weight of her position, to understand the necessity of her marriage in saving her people. She sat straighter in her seat, trying to make out, in all the rumblings, anything that could be a coherent solution.

"We are a prosperous land, but our numbers are insignificant to hold back these invaders. We are a small kingdom with few men to spare. We are farmers and craftsmen, not warriors." The room rumbled with tentative agreement. "I have brought our plight to the Kingdom of Laoch. They have agreed to lend us men as well as to train our own men to fight and defend what is ours."

Murmuring filled the air. Aoife felt the tension building like a summer storm. Curse men and their pride. She could feel the unrest coming off the men in waves. Was this why her father was tightening his hold on her freedom? What of the people in the villages? Would they learn how to protect themselves? It unsettled her but she held her tongue. She knew other men in the room were doing the same thing to not agitate the king, but that only meant they were wise, not loyal.

"What do they want in return?" one man bellowed.

Aoife felt like she was in a cramped space. These Men were too large for this room. The older men with their large bellies full of too many warm nights at home, the younger men were hard with muscle. Aoife noticed her father and his slight muscle that made him smaller than the rest. But his ability to throw his presence around the room made him seemed to make him giant-like. Perhaps this is what it meant to be king—to have power in your being, so that no matter the size or rank of a man, they followed orders.

What then, did it take to be queen?

Aoife's eyes scanned the room, she rested her gaze on three men who wore the wolf ensign she had seen the night before. As she studied the men closer, she audibly gasped. The man from the woods! His eyes met hers, as if he had heard her over all the noise. He dipped his head in a bow, his eyes full of laughter. Aoife snapped her mouth shut, composing her features. Nodding her head in return, her heart pounded, causing her to feel the pulse in her throat and making it hard to swallow.

The king raised his arms again, until the room fell back into silence. "It was easy on our end. They have a prince who will be king; he needed a wife." He shrugged his shoulders.

Aoife looked around the room and saw each man look at her in turn with a wolfish grin on his face. Her face flamed red as she tried to keep her features unreadable. She heard some men chuckle at her in response to her blush. The three young men from Laoch looked unaffected, except for the flash of the summer-sky blue eyes, who watched Aoife's face.

"We have a princess who needs a husband. This will join our kingdoms forevermore.. When my daughter marries the Prince of Laoch our troubles will be their troubles. They will aid us. It was a simple solution."

The men howled in merriment. Aoife's hands ached, she looked down and found that she was clenching them. The king had made her sound no better than a cow for sale to the highest bidder. She found herself watching the warrior whom she'd met in the woods. His mouth had turned down as he openly stared at her father. He leaned and whispered something into the ear of the large man sitting next to him who nodded solemnly.

"Stand, guests. These men will oversee all of it. Friends, daughter, meet Malcolm Cuinn." The king said.

The man who her warrior whispered too stood up. He was thick with muscle and stood taller than the rest. He had short, chestnut hair, and was, in fact, the only one in the room with short hair. Aoife had found that odd, but he had a kind face despite his brute build. King Eamonn turned to his daughter, nodding to her, his mouth turned down slightly in irritation.

Startled that her father was allowing her to greet them Aoife quickly stood and gracefully crossed over to Malcolm. He placed one hand on his chest and bowed to her. His eyes were the color of the forest.

She bowed to him as well and stated, "We are honored, Malcolm Cuinn. May our hearth warm you and our home become yours." She felt a genuine smile pull on her lips. Malcolm suddenly reached for her hand and kissed it. Bringing a chuckle from the men around them and a soft blush to her cheeks. He winked at her and released her hand.

The king, undeterred by Malcolm continued, "Liam Conaill."

The man from the woods placed his hand on his heart and bowed to her. Unlike Malcolm, he wasn't overtaken with muscles, though he was defined. His jaw was strong. His eyes were the clearest blue that Aoife had ever seen. His raven hair fell to his shoulders. He reached for her hand and her face flushed once more. She cursed herself for having all these men see her react this way. Why couldn't she control what people saw? He kissed her hand and her heart took off in a gallop.

"We are honored, Liam Conaill. May our hearth warm you and our home become yours." She was surprised at the steadiness of her voice.

In his eyes Aoife saw something, but as quickly as it came, it left. He withdrew from her.

"Killian Maoilriain, cousin to the prince." As the other two before he also grabbed her hand and placed a kiss on her knuckles. His eyes were a muddy brown, his hair the same raven's black as Liam's. His eyes were bright as if he was holding back a joke. His mouth was hard, as if his face couldn't decide what emotion he was feeling. Aoife's heart went out for him. Perhaps he was as uncomfortable as she was.

"We are honored, Killian Maoilriain. May our hearth warm you and our home become yours." she repeated a third time.

"I intend for it to be." He dropped her hand abruptly and stepped back with a hand on his chest.

Confused, Aoife glanced at the king who appeared displeased as he stared down at Killian. She went back to his side and looked again at the new men who would become her shadows. She noticed Liam wore the same expression as the king. Offended for Killian, she vowed she would make him feel welcomed despite the King and Liam Conaill's feelings towards him.

"Yes, welcome," King Eamonn said almost thoughtlessly as he sat back down staring at the new arrivals.

Music started up as the feast resumed its merriment. Talk of war faded into the night with each drink that was consumed.

Chapter 5

Shadows. That was what Aoife had gained. Everywhere she went, one of the three guards from Loach were with her, hovering behind her. It had only been one day and already Aoife found herself praying for more patience. Her jaw felt sore from the constant grinding of her teeth. She only relaxed when Maeve came, distracting her from the men. Aoife knew she should show kindness to these strangers. They were far from home after all. Maeve had forced Aoife outside to take a walk to the village and Malcolm had volunteered to be first watch. Aoife wondered if it had something to do with her friend, or if he was just eager to serve. She shrugged her shoulders, no matter. He would not have a chance with Maeve anyway. She scorned any men who tried to win her favor. Aoife always felt sorry for them, but it was entertaining to watch.

"Do you remember the plant names Rowan wanted us to recite tomorrow?" Aoife asked Maeve, as they weaved their way through the forest.

Absentmindedly, Maeve rattled off the different names and each plant's uses. She reached down and plucked a single pink flower from the bed of the roots by a tree. Plucking the petals off it one by one.

The trees' leaves were ablaze in color holding fast to the branches, determined not to fall to their deaths, the wind blew through them creating a hushing sound. It calmed Aoife's mind, which had been swirling with unwanted thoughts of the suffering of her people. It would not be fair to Maeve if Aoife's feelings of doubt ruined the afternoon.

Aoife shook her head in awe. "How do you memorize all of this? I can hardly recall the names, let alone what they look like."

Maeve shrugged her slim shoulders. "It interests me. I want to help people, if that means learning different kinds of leaves and how they are used. If that is the difference between helping someone heal or having them suffer… Well, it makes learning easy."

Maeve reached for a leaf nearest to them, plucking it from the bush. Her hands were constantly tearing at the foliage, whenever they went on their walks, as if she were incapable of keeping her hands to her side. Tearing the leaf into pieces and putting it up to her nose, sniffing the scent wafting from it, Aoife looked more closely at her friend. Maeve could have been a fairy of the woodland; her dark braid fell forward, swinging back and forth as Maeve began to fill her basket with what looked like the same leaf to Aoife.

"Tis' a shame the plants have to die for people to live," Malcolm said, intruding on their conversation. He sat leaned against a trunk, watching them both with interest.

Maeve stood up. "I suppose so, but isn't that true for all things? Death and life are an eternal circle."

"You seem not to be affected by that," Malcolm replied, pulling himself off the tree and moving towards them. His steps made no sound and Aoife wondered if that was part of the training.

He towered over the two women, filling in the peaks of sunshine with darkness. His eyes were a mixture of bottomless green and brown, as if the trees mimicked their colors after him. Maeve stood straighter, Aoife saw her eyes flash.

"Are you affected by it then? Don't you slaughter people for a living?"

Aoife's face warmed at Maeve's boldness.

Tension ripped through the air. Aoife held her breath to see how Malcolm would respond. He chuckled darkly. "True, in trying to preserve life, I often destroy it."

"A circle" Maeve nodded her head. She had lost the anger to her words after his confession.

Maeve and Malcolm would have completed a circle on their own. She brought life and tried to restore it. While no matter how kind he was, Malcolm brought death to the enemies who threatened their lives. Two halves of a whole. Both having their place in this world. Aoife kept that thought to herself though, she didn't think Maeve would appreciate it. They both had a job in the keeping the circle balanced. Aoife wondered where her place in the circle was.

"Malcolm?" Both Malcolm and Maeve twisted their heads to look at Aoife, as if remembering she was there.

Ignoring the uncomfortable feeling growing in her stomach, she continued: "What interests you Malcolm? Were you able to study herbs?" Aoife asked lamely. "Or perhaps something else?" Malcolm smirked, he rubbed his chin as if thinking hard about his answer. Maeve watched him, her eyes squinting.

"I was never one to have my nose in a book. I preferred action, learning by doing. Liam and I spent most of our time outside with a weapon in our hands. I had no patience for sitting." His face grew lighter at the memory. "Always felt more like a prison, I think my mother preferred me to be out of doors, I did less damage that way." He chuckled.

Aoife knew the feeling, a bird in a cage.

"I am much the same, though I do read. Being outside there is freedom that is hard to capture elsewhere. Is it not?" Maeve stated. Maeve picked up her basket which was now overflowing with green, Aoife's basket was bare in comparison.

"Perhaps I should start reading, any suggestions?" He winked at Maeve, her lips pinched together, turning down slightly.

Aoife winced for Malcolm. Maeve seemed to be disappointed by his question. Aoife supposed that was better than anger.

"I have no recommendations, why force yourself to read if that is not your pleasure." Maeve pivoted on her heels and turned to face the path on the way to the village. "Aoife are you coming?" Aoife smiled sympathetically at Malcolm and nodded her head as if to say come with us.

"That is too bad, it is never too late to find something surprising about yourself. Perhaps I would like reading, I just never had the time before now. How about you princess? What should I read?" Malcolm followed, unaffected by Maeve's lack of attention.

Aoife glanced behind her at Malcolm, biting her lip. "Umm...let me think on it." She glanced at Maeve, who seemed to be too preoccupied to listen.

They walked in silence until they reached the edge of the forest, Aoife could hear the rumblings of life floating across the field, a path worn down by the feet of men carved a way to the village. It was crowded today. The village was buzzing with excitement. Everyone was working in their fields, clearing away the dead crops, making room for the living ones. Collecting the crops and packing them up to be sold in the market. Children too young to work played in the center of the town.

Malcolm's stance became slightly more rigid as they entered the throng of the people. He seemed to hover closer to both Aoife and Maeve. People called out to Aoife, hailing her.

She faced Malcolm "I will be okay, these are my people."

"Noted." He winked at her, but his body stayed stiff.

"Maeve, who did you say I could buy the best fabric from? I want to buy some for the maids who serve me, they should all have fine dresses."

Maeve's eyes lit up. "Oh, you will make them the talk of the town yet."

"Do you have fabric for a new dress? Or your sisters? For the festival." Aoife asked, her eyes watching the bustle of people.

"We do not need it Aoife, don't think on us. We will be fine. Father has more than enough money."

"Alright. But let me help in this way. How can I help the village?"

"I don't think it is our village you must worry about, Saibhreas is wealthy enough, it is those from other Kingdoms that need aid."

Aoife's brow furrowed. Maeve must not have heard of the men who were coming after the kingdom.

"Maeve what do you mean?"

Her friend linked arms with Aoife to talk in her ear. "We do not trade with other villages Aoife. That is how we remain rich, but stories have been circling the village that people are dying. Crops were bad for many people, hunger creates desperate men."

"But what of their Kings? Can they not do something?" Aoife asked, tension clung to her shoulders.

"You cannot give when you do not have. Things do not come from nothing." Maeve's voice had risen slightly, excitement filling her words. "When people are desperate they do things that they would not ordinarily do."

Aoife looked at Malcolm, wondering if he would tell her father if she told Maeve about the threat coming to the kingdom. Her father had never told her not to tell anyone.

"Maeve last night my father called me to the war council. He spoke of unrest and threats coming to our town. To steal from us and do...who knows what." Aoife's mother flashed through her mind. "That is why all these men are here to protect Saibhreas, to help us protect ourselves. But perhaps there would be no violence if we gave aid. There would be no need for the exchange."

Maeve looked at her mouth curled with disgust, "Is your marriage what your father bartered with? To protect the kingdom, you must marry?"

Aoife nodded, Maeve looked at Malcolm with a cold distrust. Aoife felt sorry for him and any other man from Laoch who would run into her. Aoife wanted to redirect the conversation to save Malcolm from Maeve's wrath.

"Saibhreas should help them. I will discuss this with my father."

Maeve turned away from Malcolm and smiled, "It seems you and I both have a calling to help those who cannot help themselves."

Aoife laughed with her friend. They walked into a shop, the walls we lined with different colors and textures of fabric that it was almost as if the shop was made out of them.

A young woman came forward and clumsily curtsied at the princess.

"Princess how can I he-" Her voice caught up and she was starting behind Aoife like a fish, her mouth open. Aoife saw that she was gaping at Malcolm, his frame filled the shop. He stood like a stone though he wore an easy smile.

Maeve rolled her eyes, "Ailbe focus. Princess Aoife needs fabric for all the women who serve her at the castle."

Ailbe's silver eyes widened, her short chestnut hair fell slightly into her face. "That is very generous princess." Aoife's cheeks warmed in discomfort. "How many women serve you?"

Maeve had moved over to Malcolm. She spoke to him softly, Aoife wondered what had prompted her friend to break out of her mood.

"Twelve but cut me enough for fifteen. Just to be safe."

"Yes, we women are all different, aren't we?"

"Fortunately, we are," Aoife smiled, Ailbe seemed to have a lightness about her. "When will they be ready?"

"It is hard to say Princess, there are a lot of orders this week. Though yours will be moved to the top of the list."

"Don't do that. I just need it soon enough so that the girls can make them. It can hold."

"What color were you thinking of using?"

"Can I ask you a question?"

The young woman looks startled. "Of course!"

"Might you suggest something to me? I am not sure what they might like."

The young woman looked pleased her silver eyes sparkled with delight. She walked around the shop, touching the fabrics and comparing colors. She chatted with Aoife, talking about textures and the different kind of fabrics.

"I do want them durable though" Aoife had cut of the woman's monologue. "I want them to be able to use them for a long time."

"I think that is wise." Maeve said from the corner with Malcolm, they both were smiling. Aoife eyed her friend and Maeve waved a hand as if to say they would speak later. Aoife chuckled to herself.

Ailbe nodded her agreement and after looking back towards Malcolm one more time she went to work.

"You can send word through Maeve when they are ready. If that is alright by you both?"

Maeve nodded her head. Ailbe, now set about her task muttered her consent.

When they left the shop, the sun had begun to set, a deep pink covered the sky.

"I must go home now, I need to hang these to dry." Maeve said raising her basket in the air higher. Hugging Aoife and nodding toward Malcolm she then walked off toward her own home. What it must be like to be welcomed home every day with smiles and laughter, Aoife wondered as she watched Maeve glide into dusks' light.

Most evenings the King took his food in his chambers. The king was always planning. It did not matter, she was not usually a part of the plan. Aoife shook away the thoughts and looked to Malcolm with a smile. "Shall we too wander home?"

With a dramatic bow Malcolm gestured for her to go first. It brought a giggle from Aoife and she marched out in front, Malcolm filling the space behind her. She waved her hand to signal him forward, he came to her side, his eyes darting around everyone who passed by.

"What of your family Sir? Wouldn't you rather be home with them this evening?" She watched his face expectantly. Eager to keep the darkness in her mind at bay.

"Aye, in truth I haven't been home in a long while. In my youth I left to join with the other boys my age. I joined the warriors of my people." There was no regret in his voice, it was just a fact to his life.

"Is that what all the boys do in your kingdom? Join the warriors? Become killers early on?" There was an edge to her voice, she knew Malcolm didn't deserve the hostility, she was just curious. But she also didn't understand the need for violence, for young men to be taken from their homes to fight and kill. What was the purpose in it? Losing family should never happen to anyone. And from what Aoife had heard about the warriors of Loach, in battle they were nothing short of beasts.

Malcolm shook his head ignoring her tone. "Most men want to join. We are a large kingdom, so we need a lot of fighters. We need a lot of men who can fight. To protect what is ours. We never start a fight, but we will end one. We all have a choice. There is always a choice."

Aoife thought on that for a moment. "What of the women? What are their choices?"

They reached the entrance of the forest. The branches were like arms welcoming them in, others were trees embracing each other creating a tunnel of branches and leaves. Inviting them into the darkness. Stepping through the threshold Aoife breathed deeper, easier. It was like coming home.

His brow pinched in confusion, "They have the same choices. Some choose to join us though to fight and protect the kingdom, though it is a very small number," he chuckled, "my sister has chosen to join alongside me. She will be old enough next year."

Without being fully conscious of her actions Aoife grabbed Malcolm's arm. "You mean to tell me that girls can fight? They can do the same things that men can?"

"Yes, some of the fiercest warriors are the women. They can handle pain better than us men, well some of us men." He chuckled as if at a memory that was beyond explanation.

"I think that I will adopt that rule when I marry your prince." She grinned to herself, more freedom for everyone. *What an idea.*

"That should be no problem. It is probably on his list of changes to make already." His eyes watched before him with intensity.

"His list? How would he know what needs to be changed? He is not even here."

"He...has his eyes and ears here though."

"What do you mean?"

He turned to face her as if to make his point clear. "I cannot say much more. He is serious about his duties. You and this kingdom have become a priority of his. Know that he will do his best to serve you both." His voice had a finality to it. Aoife didn't know Malcolm, but she had a feeling she better not press the point.

What was that supposed to mean? She knew he was serious about not saying anything more. That bothered her, was she always to be in the darkness of ignorance?

"You said you have a sister? Do you have any other siblings?"

He seemed grateful to her for changing the subject.

The rest of the walk was filled with Malcolm telling stories of his past. Aoife tried to focus on what he was saying, her mind kept reverting back to what Malcolm had said. Her heart knocked against her rib cage like an anxious guest at the door.

The pink of the sky melted into a deep blue when they arrived back at the castle. Shadows and light melted together.

"Shall we be friends?" Aoife asked reaching out her hand to his before they reached the gate. He gripped her small hand into his, "Friends."

As if appearing from the very darkness itself Killian emerged. "Time to trade Malcolm, Liam needs you."

Aoife jumped in surprise, but Malcolm seemed to be expecting it. Malcolm bowed and started off to the courtyard where the clashing of swords could be heard. Aoife smiled at Killian and started to retreat to her room.

Perhaps her new shadows would become friends after all.

Chapter 6

The sounds of men grunting and metal clanging on metal reached Aoife's ears. Aoife looked onward at Maeve and Rowan, neither of whom seemed disturbed by the noise. Aoife hoped that Malcolm would be the one on guard duty with her for the evening. Malcolm was becoming less of a shadow and more of a friend. He had an easy personality to him, he was relaxed and alert. Killian and Liam teetered between shadows and clarity, it was if they preferred to remain slightly aback from it all, unfocused. Aoife shuddered at the cold chill that filled the room and leaned forward pushing away the noise of the soldiers.

"... that is the most effective way to gather the grain from the fields." Rowan ended, crossing his hands together in front of him. Sweat dripped from his receding hairline as like it was the fountain of knowledge pouring from his head. Maeve was nodding her head slowly no doubt retaining all the information Rowan just prattled on about.

"I will have to tell my father, he will be grateful to keep more grain than in the past years," Maeve said, excitement lighting up her face.

Rowan smiled pleased at his beloved pupil, drinking in the knowledge. Maeve was always the one to love learning, Aoife found it all tolerable, but she longed more to be roaming outdoors then stuck with a stuffy man who didn't seem to like her anyways. Aoife was grateful that Maeve was with her for the lessons, it allowed Aoife time for her day dreams, Aoife really didn't like being the center of attention. It was hard to avoid as royalty, but she did well for herself. It was easier for her to be in a crowd, forgotten, that way she could see people more clearly. Perhaps that is why Liam and Malcolm also kept themselves apart from her.

Rowan glanced toward Aoife who had returned her attention toward the window, listening to the sounds of training men and the sharp breeze running through the air. His smile dropped into a passive expression, he rose from his seat murmuring to himself as he walked among the bookshelves. The room smelled of paper and dust. It was lined with stacks of books in disarray.

Maeve tapped Aoife's arm dragging her attention away from the outside world.

"If your father implemented these ideas, our kingdom would be able to produce more, not just for our people. But for the surrounding Kingdoms and tribes as well."

Aoife stared into the face of her friend, passion seeped from her voice. Aoife was amazed at Maeve, always thinking of other people. Shame filled Aoife, Maeve would be the better queen.

"Do you believe other villages need help?" She asked naively, realizing that Maeve was waiting for a response.

Maeve's brow pinched as she cocked her head, she looked disappointed. "Aoife, suffering is universal. Not all people are as well off as we. There is always more to be done to... to help."

Guilt swept through Aoife, she patted her friends' arm. "You are wise, I will suggest Rowan bring it up to the King."

"Do you think he will listen?"

"King Eamonn?"

Maeve nodded hope filling her eyes.

Rowan came back, allowing Aoife the excuse of not having to answer. In her heart she doubted that her father would change anything about the production of Saibhreas, or that he would listen to anyone who would try and convince him. Her father knew what he wanted, and it prospered Saibhreas, but growth cannot be found without change.

Rowan had arms filled with books of all sizes. All seemed to be containing information on harvesting. He laid them out in front of the girls. Aoife groaned, she loved to read of love and adventure. Not on how one would best plant crops.

"Pick two and read them by the end of this week. The point of reading is to gain knowledge, not to entertain you," he looked pointedly at Aoife. "They are more valuable to you for that reason, pick wisely."

With books in her hands Maeve made her way towards the door, stopping to wait for Aoife. However, Aoife was slower about choosing her form of torture. None of them were small enough to be read in an afternoon. Accepting her fate she grabbed her books, heading to the door she was almost to freedom when she heard Rowan's nasally voice.

"Princess Aoife will you remain behind. There is something I wish to discuss with you." Rowan took the remaining books and put them back on the shelves.

Maeve collected her books and with a reassuring smile shrugged her shoulders. "I will wait for you outside?" Maeve asked, looking towards the sky.

Aoife knew Maeve was calculating when she needed to be home and when the sun would start to set. Aoife shook her head, "I will see you tomorrow?"

Maeve nodded looking relieved and winked at Aoife before she left the room.

Silence filled the air, weighing heavy on Aoife's mind.

"Princess Aoife, I realize that outside might be more appealing than this room. However, that does not mean that you can slack off. Soon you will be queen and as queen you need to know how to help your people," Rowan scolded. His already red face seemed to glow brighter. The roots of agitation and guilt grew in Aoife until it blossomed on her face in shades of pink.

Rowan sighed heavily and shook his head. He went to a shelf that contained different objects and pulled out a dusty box. It had carvings of ancient symbols on it. Aoife could hear him muttering to himself, something about her lack of focus and self-control. The heat in her face flamed anew, tears threatened in the back of her throat. Why did she always mess up? It seemed that today was only for reminders of how unworthy she was to do anything, she was to be queen, but was she really made to be queen. Her mother was intelligent and graceful and kind. Aoife felt that her mother would not be pleased with how she was behaving. She fought the beast of pity that formed in her belly, warning her that she was about to be consumed.

"You are dismissed child." As gracefully as she could she stood, picking up the books that Rowan had assigned for her to read and left the room. Shutting the door behind her and leaning against it she pressed her fingers tightly to the bridge of her nose to keep from screaming or crying. She wasn't sure which force would be the more powerful force inside her that would break open first. All she wanted was to spend the afternoon dictating herself and her own actions. Not being led and told what to do by old men or being confronted about her faults.

Aoife stood straight and glanced around to see if her shadows had emerged for the day. No one was in the corridor, she felt her mouth raise itself into a grin. Of course, they wouldn't be here, she thought, her lessons with Rowan still had an hour more. A perfect head start, she practically ran to her room casting the books on her bed.

She grabbed her cloak from her wardrobe fastening the scarlet strings around her neck. Aoife nearly skipped down the halls, her mood improving all the way to the entrance of the woods. Putting up her hood to hide the castle from her view.

"I must leave the path today father." She whispered as she walked off the known, used path onto a new path, her own path.

***

Before Aoife's mother was taken, they used to explore the wilderness surrounding the palace together. Saibhreas was a land filled with trees until her father insisted that the majority of it was cut down and sold. Now all that remained of the once great forest was the trees that surrounded the castle.

Aoife could remember her mother's hair down, flying with the wind as they explored through the woods, that is how they came to find their place. No one knew of it, not even the king. It was their secret place, hidden deep in the forest. The branches were knit closely together, shielding off intruders from entering it.

Aoife rarely came here anymore, only when she needed to feel close to her mother, when days were especially hard. She had told Maeve of this place but never took her here. Now it was hers alone. She avoided the place, in case anyone followed her or looked for her. Aoife breathed in deeply the musk of wet wood and pine that hung in the air. Creatures chattered noisily with each other, allowing her to blend in with them, as if she too were a creature of the forest. The thought made Aoife smile. If only she could stay here forever. She loosened her braid, letting her pale wavy hair falling around her.

She looked around at the little alcove of trees, it was a perfect circle outlined in trees with the thickest branches, closing a curtain all around her. Enveloping her in their secret places. A small pond lay in the middle of the area, stones surrounded it in what looked like the shape of a wheel and by it was a lone tree with low hanging branches and a wide welcoming trunk. Aoife thought that the branches were perfect sitting places, and though she would stay on the ground, she thought Maeve would appreciate the tree. One day she would share this place with someone.

Today it was her own. She grabbed the small book she kept in the pocket of her skirts and sat at the base of the tree. Facing the pond and began to read. The damp air settled on her from the trees, she shivered. Losing herself to the words on the pages, and the safety she felt in the trees.

***

SNAP.

Aoife woke with a start. She held her breath as she heard soft steps fall on the branches. Hair raised on the back of her neck. Before she could see the intruder, she heard a deep tenor voice.

"A new book already?"

Aoife scrambled to her feet, her hair falling wildly to her waist. Liam?

Her heart beat rapidly in her chest, her breath coming out short.

"How did you find me?" She asked. Fury rattled in her bones. She felt exposed, as if someone had cut her open and looked inside her. She looked around for his friends, for anyone else who might have come with him. Cursing to herself.

"I am alone, "his voice was even, ignoring her first question. He was telling her the truth. It startled her, how easily he read her thoughts. Though she was never good at deceiving.

"How did you find me?" She repeated, her voice clipped. Panic gripped her, then her anger burned it away.

Liam would tell her father she was far from the trail. She looked to the sky and saw the gray of dusk falling around them. She had lost track of time. How many more men were searching for her?

So careless!

He looked at her, his sky-blue eyes assessing her movements. He raised his brow in confusion. It gave Aoife some pleasure to know that though he seemed to know her thoughts, he didn't know the reasons behind them.

"Think Princess. How is any prey caught?" He shrugged his shoulders, his voice light.

Was...was he teasing her?

She studied him, and she knew he was assessing her as well. He was calm, though there was a rigidness to his body to let her know that he was alert. He seemed unaffected by her anger.

Of course! His sole purpose for being here was not to watch after her, it was to lead the King's soldiers to become like the warriors of Laoch. The stories speak of the warriors who turned into beasts in battle. Men who would tear an enemy apart with his teeth if necessary.

Malcolm had once told her that Liam was the best warrior that Laoch had. She wondered if he was even better than her betrothed.

"Did you...did you track me?!" her voice went high at the end. She felt like laughing and crying all at once. He had hunted her like an animal.

"In a sense. Everyone leaves a trail, whether they know it or not." A small smile grew at his lips as if he had a private joke. "Come princess, I must return you home or your father will inquire after you."

"The King doesn't know I left?"

"I didn't have the chance to tell anyone." He shrugged his shoulders. "There wasn't a sign of struggle, I figured you left on your own. You seem more comfortable with the woods than with people."

"They are more reliable than people," she murmured to herself.

He nodded and stepped forward, removing a fallen twig from her hair. She felt her face flush as he stepped away, heading back to the entrance he had made for himself.

Hope flamed inside her, if he hadn't told anyone there was still a chance that it could remain hers only.

"Liam?" she called and walked toward him closing the distance between them. "Please don't tell anyone about this place," she gestured around her. "No one... knows of this place, especially my father. I want to keep it this way. Please."

She knew a princess shouldn't beg, but she needed him to know this was important to her. Perhaps she could resonate with his heart rather than his duty. She twisted her hands behind her back while he stared at her. As if he were trying to see her, she pushed away her urge to squirm and lifted her chin, looking him in the eyes.

Without thinking she reached for his hands, wrapping them in her own. He needed to understand. His hands were rough like the bark on a tree, from years of swordplay no doubt. He was a trained killer after all. His clear blue eyes held hers as if searching her mind for the desperation she showed. He pulled one hand out of her grasp and reached up to pull another twig from her hair. She tried not to flinch away from him.

"I will keep your secret Princess," he sighed.

Relief washed over her.

"Thank you, Liam," she smiled at him, her heart slowing its pace, "and please, call me Aoife. We have a shared secret, which makes us friends."

She knew she was smiling like a fool, but she couldn't help it. She felt that deep down she could trust Liam. That he was the type of man who keeps his word. It scared her that it came so naturally to her. She shook away the thought, it was because Malcolm trusted him, that was all.

His sky-blue eyes widened at her words, a small smile played at his lips. He squeezed her hand, and then let go. Her face flamed in response. How silly of her to hold his hand! What was she thinking, she was going to marry his future king? He really must think that she was no more than a silly girl.

They walked out of her hidden haven in silence, reaching the path that led her directly home. The path her father cautioned her to never leave.

Chapter 7

Aoife silently thanked Liam again for keeping his mouth shut about going in search for her as she quickly braided her hair, pulling the last few leaves out of her hair. For the first time since her shadows arrived she felt relief and comfortable. She looked at the man in front of her, his black hair falling to his shoulders in a wild manner. He walked with authority, but he promised to keep her secret. Perhaps being in authority didn't mean you had to be domineering as well.

"Liam, do you miss your family?" She asked, catching up to him. He didn't turn to acknowledge her but answered her.

"I suppose I do. But it is nice to be outside Laoch walls and see something different." Liam had an easy smile and Aoife felt her own mouth mirroring his. It was easy to feel lighter in his presence. Normally with his men Liam looked so...serious.

"What does Laoch look like? What are the people like? What is your story?" Aoife inquired.

"I don't have a story Princess. Besides haven't you read about it yet in those books of yours? I am sure you could tell me more about my home then I ever could."

"How can that be? You have eyes, don't you?"

Liam chuckled, and Aoife felt her face flame. She was shocked by her own bluntness.

"Aye Aoife, but my eyes were set upon weapons, there was never time for anything else."

"Wouldn't you ever...have fun?"

He grinned, "That is fun to me. Nothing greater than swordplay. You'll see."

Aoife snorted. "The King would never let me."

Servants shuffled past them as they made their way through the halls towards Aoife's room.

"You have a story Liam, everyone does. Most people aren't patient enough to listen." She stood to face him, her face eager. "Books can give you a lot, but human experience gives us more."

His eyes took her in, examining her open face. He stopped in front of her door. She didn't know what he was searching for, but his smile widened. He crossed his arms over his chest, leaning against the wall for support.

"The castle sits on the edge of a cliff. Below the cliff lies sand and the sea." He went quiet and Aoife saw his eyes glaze over, as if he could see his home now before him. "The village lies beyond the castle, it hums with life. People fill the streets, there is hardly room to breathe, but the land of Laoch goes on forever. That is all I know really, too busy playing in the armory for other details." His eyes narrowed at the thought and Aoife wondered if he liked fighting or if he learned to fight and out of duty and service to his King and people.

Like her duty would be to marry his prince.

"Tell me Liam, what is your prince like?" She tried to act uninterested so as not to give herself away.

He blinked as if he were just waking. Then a wolfish smile curled about his lips. "Oh him? He is alright, so far as princes go. I hear that he throws tantrums like a child when he doesn't get his way. Runs to his mother and cries."

Bewilderment covered the princess' face before she could contain her emotions. Liam started laughing.

"Are you mocking me?" her hands flew to her hips and she could feel her face grow hot.

"No, it was just your face. You should have seen it," he chuckled again. Aoife could feel her anger boil.

"Well sir, I do not know if you were ever taught this by your mother. But for one, girls do not appreciate being toyed with, and for another they do not like having their faces laughed at," Her voice came in clipped tones.

The humor fled from his face, but a small smile remained. His eyes flashed with merriment which only added to Aoife's annoyance.

"Aye princess, my mother did warn me. But having a good laugh is not going to kill you."

Without another word she pivoted away from him, her face flushing.

"Where you are going?" He called.

At least he had the common sense to stay where he was.

"To the kitchen! I am hungry."

She didn't look back. A voice crept to her that it was a mistake to let Liam into her life, that it was not going to end well for her. She raised her eyes to the ceiling and prayed that Liam could be trusted to keep her secret.

Chapter 8

The staff was bustling about, preparing various meats for the king and his guests. It was stifling hot in the kitchen and Aoife wondered how the cooks could bare it day after day. The kitchens smelled of cinnamon and it filled her nostrils with every breath she took.

When the cooks saw her, they bowed slightly and acknowledged her, but quickly they set back to their tasks. Aoife liked that best, when people did not treat as though she were special. She chose an open chair in the corner of the room and sat down, out of the way of the workers.

Her father for the last week, every night, had eaten his meals with his war council. Rumors fluttered around the kitchen of tribes on the borders growing restless, attacking villagers in the further parts of the land. Aoife was secretly glad there were invaders. She knew that perhaps that was evil. But it gave her father a greater purpose. He was more alive than usual. Sometimes the greatest heartaches can be blessings in disguise. She thought to herself, she doubted that if she said it out loud that anyone would agree with her.

She shook the thoughts away from her mind and looked at the barrel of apples next to her. She helped herself to one and watched the cooks weaving in and out between each other, it was an odd dance. They could anticipate where the other was going to step. And it was mesmerizing to watch with the fire lights behind them causing their shadows to stretch across the wall and flicker in and out her sight. The longer she watched them the more real they became. It was as if they had come to life on their own and beckoned for Aoife to join them.

Scoffing to herself she cast if off from her mind as fairy tricks. The warmth of the room curled about her like a blanket, her eyes fluttered open and shut. She rested her head back against the stone wall.

"Princess?" A deep male voice was speaking to her. "Princess." A gruff voice spoke again. Aoife gasped and jumped forward, she was so surprised she almost smacked her forehead into Killian's chin. Why did she keep falling asleep? It was comfortable here, she reminded herself.

He leaned near her and was now too close to her face. Heat flowered on her cheeks and she was grateful for the dim light of the fire to hide the flush of her face.

"Princess your father is summoning you," he sounded irritated.

His body was tense and rigid, just like Liam and Malcolm. They always seemed ready for a fight. She felt bad that he was forced to become one of her shadows. She could tell he did not like it at all. Not that the others did, she quickly added to herself. But whereas Malcolm was a fast friend and Liam, hopefully, tolerated her, Killian never seemed to warm to her, no matter how hard she tried. This was the longest conversation Killian had had with her.

He stood up and walked to the entrance of the kitchen. Aoife was still a little dazed from waking up so abruptly. She stood and looked around the room, the fires had lulled to a dull roar. And the cooks were nowhere to be seen. They probably were eating their own meals. She heard a click of a tongue and sigh from Killian.

Aoife could feel the embarrassment within her swell. She swallowed it back down. She put a small smile on her face and headed in his direction.

"I am sorry that you had to come fetch me," he was silent. He moved quickly that Aoife felt she had to almost run to keep up with the pace he was setting. "Are you finding your stay here pleasant?" she tried again.

Silence.

"Did you spend your day training?" She knew she was asking silly questions, but she wanted to try to be his friend. He had come a long way from his home to watch her on orders of his king. Not by his own choice, he was trained for war, not for watching after a princess. She felt she could relate to him, as a warrior your choices were made for you in battle. He still said nothing.

"One of these days I would like to watch the training. See what is being taught." When he still said nothing, she tried the only thing she could think of that would get a response from a man, "Perhaps I will join."

He scoffed at her and turned to face her. Got him, she thought. "Women are not taught to fight. They are protected."

"Perhaps that should change. What if anything happened to all the men, what would the women do? Cower before the invaders? Or they could fight alongside their men and help. Besides Malcolm told me that Laoch offers this chance to their women."

He openly laughed at her, it was a cruel sound. "They would be slaughtered before they could raise their swords. They would also distract the men. Battle is no place for women, Princess. They would end up hindering any cause they were on. I have that knowledge from experience," he smirked.

She sighed to herself, the ignorance of men was going to be her undoing. She had to smile inwardly, she got him to talk. She counted that as a small victory. Though she was not sure, if it could really count as a victory.

"Then where would you say a woman's place is sir? In a home? Waiting to see whether her husband will walk through the door or an invader? That seems silly to me. When I am queen…"

Killian whipped around and gripped her by the arm. She let out a yelp in surprise at his suddenness.

"Yes, but don't you see princess," he sneered. "You will be under the rule of your king, your husband. He will tell you what to do.

And if I know my cousin, the prince, he will not have a woman telling him how to run his throne."

He let her go and continued to walk to the dining hall. She rubbed her arm where he had grabbed. She wondered if it was going to bruise.

Who was this prince she is supposed to marry? Was he a child? Or a hard-hearted fool?

Killian had opened the door for her to enter. She set her shoulders back and placed a warm smile on her face. Not wanting Killian to see how he rattled her. She entered with all the dignity she could muster. The voices in the room cut off into silence. She nodded her head toward the men who stood for her as she entered. She looked as many as she could in the eye. She took her seat next to her father and waited for the noise to resume.

She was not sure why she had been summoned, but she was grateful for the company. The room smelled of sweat and meat, the stench made Aoife's stomach queasy. She sipped on the port given her while twisting her food around the plate. The men in the room grumbled at each other, noise rattling around her ears.

She looked across the room. Killian had joined Liam and Malcolm. While they conversed, Killian sat observing his surroundings, not talking to anyone tearing at his meat. Liam's hair had been tied in a knot behind him, she thought that he looked better with it flowing wildly, then when it was contained. Malcolm seemed to be telling him something important when they both looked over at her. She nodded in their direction.

Aoife looked at her father, his hands clasped in front of him. He looked exhausted, time and grief had worn him away into the man who was before her.

"Father why am I here?"

Silence followed. She looked quickly at Liam cursing him. He watched, a smile covering his features. Her own smile dropped into a grimace.

"Rowan tells me that you were distracted today Aoife?" he sounded tired.

Her face flushed. Drat Rowan. "I-" Her voice died as he turned to face her.

"Don't disappoint me Aoife. If you choose to be distracted I shall have Maeve banned from studies with you."

Her heart pounded in her ears and tears sprang to her eyes. Surely, he did not mean that. He would not send her only friend away.

"I understand my king. Forgive me." She bowed slightly to the King.

She blinked hard and looked forward, the food was being cleared away. She felt eyes upon her face, she turned to see Liam looking on her. His expression had hardened. She needed to be careful not to provoke the king.

"Daughter, you will stay until I dismiss you. This is for you to hear and learn from." The King said, he raised his hands above his head. Almost instantly silence filled the room. He stood, turning toward the men from Laoch.

"Sir Conaill, how are the men adjusting to your command? Are they ready?" All eyes turned to Liam.

Liam stood as well, "All good things take time. However, time is a luxury. By the end of this month your men would be almost as good as mine." He bowed sitting back down.

The King nodded his iron eyes flashed in pride.

"Caelan what of the borders?"

A tall, fat man stood. His beard was braided and tied off at the end. His teeth yellowed as he grinned wolfishly. He must oversee border protection Aoife thought.

"Many are attempting to enter into the borders of Saibhreas. There are reports of failed crops and loss livestock. Our men have held them off, but their numbers are growing more rapidly. If young Conaill will have his people send more reinforcements we can hold off better."

This must be what the kitchen was rumbling about. Aoife remembered what Maeve had said to her earlier about suffering of others. With all the courage she could muster Aoife stood up. She coughed into her hand, gaining attention that normally she would give anything to keep away from her.

"Would it not be...better if we were to help them? Give them the food and safety they seek. Then they would not get violent. Saibhreas surely has more than enough resources..." Aoife's voice died off.

The King's eyes glared, Aoife could feel the bile rising in her throat.

"Let them in here and our own people starve!" One man shouted.

"They are leeches, the lot of them. Let them figure out their own way," another man shouted.

"Any for them means less for us!"

This caused the room to burst out in heated cries. The king raised his arms again, silence reluctantly followed.

"My king, you told me that I am to marry the prince of Laoch because we need protection, correct?" Aoife continued when the king said nothing. "We have greater resources between the two kingdoms to protect those who cannot protect themselves. There are more of us than them. If we just-"

"Silence girl!" A man sneered. "You know noth-" his voice was cut off as Aoife saw Liam grab a hold of him by his collar.

His eyes flashed in anger, "hold your tongue fool." He let the young boy down and Aoife watched as fear entered the young boys' eyes. "As representatives for the king of Laoch, I would like to hear what Princess Aoife suggests."

"As would I," Malcolm winked at Aoife.

Aoife looked toward the king to see if she should continue. the king wore a blank expression.

Aoife swallowed her fear. "If we take on the surrounding tribes, they would be in our debt, the threat would diminish. Send for the scribe Rowan, father, let him tell you how we can increase the quantity of our own crops as to have enough to have plenty for our people and to help those around us."

Liam nodded in approval.

The king looked at the princess and said, "Send for the scribe Rowan."

Chapter 9

The book Rowan asked her to read, slid from her hands to the floor, her mind was far away. A knock sounded on her door, but it was drowned out by the thoughts swimming in her head.

Did that all happen last night? The king had listened with interest to Rowan. Her father put Rowan as in overseer to harvesting the crops in the kingdom. The other leaders of the kingdom seemed to be pacified, even the king seemed more pleases than normal. The season was too late for this year, but next year they would give aid to the bordering tribes. Aoife was pleased that King Eamonn had listened and that change would be made, but would it be too late? Would any of this satisfy the people long enough?

A knock again sounded at her door. She crossed to it opening the door a crack, just enough to see her face, her hair fell around her in a tangle of gold around her waist. Dark eyes met hers through the slit in the door.

"Killian, what-"

"Get dressed quickly. I have a surprise for you. You have to come with me quickly."

"Killian I am not- "

"Look I thought a lot about what you said last night. I am sorry for how I acted. I think it would be good for you to see the warriors of your kingdom train. I changed my mind. But you have to come with me now, before the guard switches and more servants arise from their beds." There was an energy to him now that he didn't have yesterday. Was this the same person?

She pulled on her simple blue frock and left with Killian. They walked quickly through the halls. They arrived at the open courtyard, a light rain had started. He put his finger to his mouth to warn her to be quiet.

"Its beginning," he gestured to the floor below them. The courtyard was spacious. Dozens of men all stood erectly, eyes forward. Aoife glanced her eyes in the same position. Trying to see what they were looking at.

Liam stood in front, staring into their faces. He had a tightness in his stance. He put his arm across his chest resting his knuckles over his heart.

"Every part of you is a weapon. When you fight, use everything you have. Fight until there is nothing left to give, fight until you are broken. And keep fighting after that. Never show weakness and never give up, not until your last breath."

He spoke with authority, leaving no room for interpretation. He exuded confidence. She looked at the men and saw the pride set in their shoulders the arms also resting across their chests.

They shifted ever so silently, anticipation to fight flowed through their veins and pumped their heart full of life.

Liam continued, "men of Saibhreas, your duty is to your brothers who share this land with you. Your loyalty is to King Eamonn and his daughter, Princess Aoife. You will give every breath to ensure the safety of their people, of your people." His blue eyes flashed, a wolfish grin planted on his face.

The men put fists over their hearts, all shouting in agreement.

Aoife smiled, she could see their eyes shine with respect and anticipation for the fight that awaited them, their energy seemed to pound in her. Liam looked around the room and nodded to Malcolm.

"Begin!" Malcolm shouted.

Aoife was mesmerized at the movements that followed, every man moved with grace and power. Each had their eyes flashing with every ring of their swords. From time to time Liam would call out an order. The men who obeyed gained ground over their opponent.

"Liam is a natural leader." She whispered, in awe.

She looked over to Killian his face seemed to be half in shadow. His eyes were as hard as steel as he watched the training.

"Perhaps he is simply a good liar," he glanced at her.

Killian seemed to have a bad opinion of everyone. First her betrothed and now Liam. She stared at him, trying to figure him out. She didn't need to know all his judgement. It didn't help her to like him much. Killian thought very highly of himself, men like that could be dangerous, she resisted the urge to roll her eyes.

"You know Killian, he is human and maybe he lies. But he was born a leader, there is no faking that."

I have tried, she thought to herself. His brow furrowed deeper and he refused to look at her. She focused back on Liam and the men below them, she didn't know anything about the men who had become her shadows. But Liam had kept her secret, no matter what else he she knew she could trust him. With that he had earned her loyalty.

Liam was looking around the room, his blue eyes observing every move, as if he could see everyone and everything they did. His black hair fell loosely about his emotionless face. Did he ever openly showed emotion? Or if he found it better to hide away that part of him? Aoife felt a pang of jealousy, she had never learned to master her emotions, to give nothing away.

Since the death of her mother, she decided instead to only ever smile, that way everyone would think she was the happy and complacent princess they expected her to be. She even could fool the king and pretend that she was content with her life. Only Maeve had ever seen her cry after her mother's death, only Maeve could see her truly. But still other emotions slipped out of the box she tried to lock inside herself and they would reveal themselves on her face. She focused again on Liam and she nearly gasped out loud, those clear blue eyes were staring directly at her.

She felt herself flush, she wondered now if she wasn't supposed to be there. It had never crossed her mind that she was not allowed somewhere in her own home. But then again, she supposed that most men would find a woman too delicate to be witnessing these situations. She held herself from shrinking back under his stare. And she produced a small smile as a peace offering. She saw his mouth twitch before his eyes flicked to Killian next to her. She thought she could hear his jaw snap shut.

She glanced at Killian and saw him smiling down at Liam as if he had something over on him. A deep sound rumbled in Killian's chest. like a dog who growls over his territory. She gripped his arm and felt Liam's stare snap in her direction. Killian bore his teeth in a shape of a smile.

"Killian I must leave, I have studies," she stood up and without looking back at either one of them, she walked out. Aoife could feel Liam's eyes following her as she went.

***

Maeve was already in the room when Aoife got there. No sign of Rowan. Maeve's deep brown hair was braided down her back and small white flowers woven into the braid. Her fair skin seemed to make her eyes a deep black this morning. She was hunched over a book weaving something in her hands and humming to herself.

"What are you doing?" Aoife asked.

Maeve turned to face her friend, smiling. "Meara put flowers in my hair this morning. Wanted me to look my best for the princess." She rolled her eyes as Aoife giggled. "I wanted to make her a little crown of some flowers to wear."

Aoife laughed at the thought of the little sister of Maeve wearing a crown of flowers. "She will be the envy of all her friends."

"Before I forget, Ailbe said that your fabric was ready to be picked up, if you wanted to come with me to the village after."

"I could use a good walk. Oh, Maeve I must tell you of last night! I went to the council room with my father and I-"

"Enough chattering girls. Let us begin." Rowan stepped into the room from the hall. Though he was the one late for the lecture, he treated them as though they were the ones intruding on his time.

Chapter 10

Harvest was a few weeks away which meant that Aoife would see her friend less often. Maeve's father was a harvester and all hands were needed to collect all the grain. Aoife couldn't stop herself from waiting though. All of last week and Aoife had not seen any sign of Maeve, just as she was about to turn around and to go inside the castle alone, she saw, emerging from the trees like a fairy queen, Maeve. Her dark brown hair was waving slightly with the leaves in the wind.

Aoife grinned and waved enthusiastically at her friend. Calling to her, Maeve returned the smile and it lit up her whole face, making her fairy beauty even more enchanting. The girls linked arms.

"Maeve I am so glad you are back, I swear Rowan almost waited here with me. Lessons aren't the same without you, Rowan doesn't try as hard, no one to impress. How is your family? Are your crops doing well?"

They walked past the gate into the castle nodding people along the way.

"Everything is well. My father said I could come today since I wouldn't leave him alone about being here. He tried to tell me crops were more important than lessons with Rowan," her eyes sparked as she rolled them.

Aoife laughed, delighted to have her friend back, "what did you say?"

A spark flickered and ignited in her deep brown eyes. "I simply told him that if that was true that I would not be mothering him. However, if Caoimhe or any other one of my siblings were to get sick who could help them better than me? And what if Rowan had taught that day something that could save them and yet unfortunately I was with him cutting grain."

"He would be very sorry because he would have to listen to you tell him so for the rest of his life." Aoife giggled.

Maeve laughed at that and nodded seriously. "It is in everyone's best interest to let me have my way. Well at least for this," she looked around, "where are your shadows today, have they given up following you around?"

"I am not so lucky. They are just better at hiding," she nodded toward the doors of the castle. In the passageway an outline of a man filled the space. "Malcolm is my shadow today. I think he might be just a little less happy than I that you have returned," her friend rolled her eyes again and sighed.

"Well he can be rest assured that I only missed you." The girls giggled and headed toward the study arm in arm.

***

After the lesson with Rowan, Maeve stayed until dusk. They walked around the castle's grounds and laughed the day away. Aoife felt lighter when Maeve was with her. Maeve brought light and freedom with her.

It all ended too soon when Maeve said with a sigh, "I must go, or my brothers will come looking for me."

"Perhaps my shadows would send them away and you could stay with me." Aoife smiled not looked at her friend, she knew she sounded desperate. She hated that she relied on Maeve.

Maeve stared at Aoife, but the princess refused to return the gaze. She knew her eyes would give away the truth that she was trying to hide. Her face was flushed as she grew irritated with herself. Maeve gripped her hand and let the silence weave in between them. As the oldest of seven, Maeve was used to comforting younger siblings. Her shoulder was permanently worn down from being leaned on. Aoife didn't want to weary her with one more problem.

"I can have Malcolm walk you back, if that will make your family more comfortable." Aoife said cheerfully, changing the subject.

Maeve scoffed "I know these woods better than he, I will be fine."

"Will you come tomorrow?" Aoife replied distracted. Maeve's deep eyes searched hers. She must have found something concerning because she softened her voice "Aye, I will be back."

"Be safe," Aoife said as she watched her friend walk into the arms of the trees and fade from view behind the branches.

"Your friend is a pretty one," a deep voice traveled from the darkness. Malcolm appeared next to her, the moonlight laying across him, giving him a silver glow to his impish smile. She looked up at him and the humor shone brightly on her face.

"Hmm... if you want a chance you should learn her mind," Aoife winked at him. His face became thoughtful and she widened her smile. *That will be interesting to watch* she thought to herself.

"I am glad she will be returning," another deep voice sounded on the other side of Aoife. She jumped at the tenor voice, Liam was painted in shadows, his face was hard to read. She felt a blush travel from her head to her toes. Her stomach danced with the rhythm of his voice. *Great, two big oafs are going to fight for my friend.* "you laugh more with her."

Aoife was startled, her heart pounded in her chest. *He noticed that?* Her face flamed once more, and she hoped that the moon's light would not expose her.

"You are very...observant," she said lamely, her voice was caught in her throat. His eyes twinkled at her and she felt as if he were grinning at her from his cover of darkness. *Could he see through her?*

Aoife excused herself and went to her room. Hours ticked by and no matter how much she tried to focus on the book in her hand, her thoughts persistently went back to the previous week and Liam. *Was Liam someone she could really trust?* She felt that maybe she could. After all he was there for her protection. Ridiculous she thought to herself, he was to protect her from physical danger, her heart was for her to protect. She fell asleep thinking of Liam.

    ***

Aoife awoke, her floorboards groaning, the hairs raised on the back of her neck. Her floor only protested when someone walked over by the window. She opened her eyes, blackness lay sprawled in all the corners of the room. It was too early for Neasa to be in her room, the castle should be asleep except for the guards. She forced herself to remain still so as not to alert whoever was in the room. She thought that maybe she made it up in her mind, she tried to relax but something inside her screamed that something was off. She stifled her breathing so as to hear better, letting herself hear the story that silence would tell her. Perhaps it was all in her head, she shifted slightly in her bed and she could hear an intake of breath.

Aoife pressed her eyes tightly shut, her mind was whirling of possibilities. Maybe a maid was stoking the fire. Yes, that is what it had to be, she was safe in her room. Someone would be outside watching her door. In that moment she felt a cool breeze tickle her cheek and exposed arms.

Aoife didn't remember opening up the window. Trepidation filled her body in waves. The cool air was suddenly cut off. She could hear the shallow breathing again it sounded closer to her this time.

Aoife sat straight up in her bed, scrambling to the end of her bed. "LI-"

A hand smacked against her mouth, stopping all sound. Her lips cut on her teeth drawing blood. In a snake like grip she was thrown against the chest of her capture, one hand pressed firmly against her mouth. She thrashed around in the tight hold, trying to cause any room for escape. The man behind her grunted his grip tightening not anticipating that the princess would put up a fight.

He slammed her back against the wall, his hold on her mouth never loosening. He was a big man, but she didn't recognize him. The blackness drenched her sight. Terror seized her body, she felt the crisp air from the outside dancing around her skirt. She was near her window. Was he to throw her out?

She had to alert the guard outside her door. Liam's voice filled her head, *every part of you is a weapon. Fight until there is nothing left to give.* Her eyes darted about the room. Next to her was a table with her water pitcher on it, empty. She went slack in her attacker's hands, hoping he would think she was giving up.

She breathed deeply and shook her shoulders more fiercely, like a scared animal who was cornered. It felt like an eternity, but the pressure she felt on her arms and back slackened slightly. Using this momentum, she pushed into him catching him off guard, causing him to stumble backwards.

She lost her balance and had to throw her body to the side, slamming her ribs into the table, knocking the air from her lungs.

The man recovered quickly and started for her, he grabbed her by her arms and started to drag her again towards the window. In a last effort she kicked her feet into the table again, knocking the glass pitcher to the floor.

Aoife's heart raced in her chest, her breath coming out in gasps, the door swung open, Killian filled the door frame. In his panic her attacker shoved her forward and she fell colliding into the shelf once more before landing in the puddle of glass. It cut into her soft flesh, causing her to cry out in shock and pain.

In her panic she forced herself off the ground ignoring the protesting screams of her ribs and legs to stand behind Killian. Putting distance between her and her attacker.

The man was quick, as Killian drew his sword, the man jumped out the window. Killian swore and ran to the window himself. She gripped her side putting pressure on it hoping the pain would stop, her breath came out in short bursts. Her legs and hands pulsed with pain. Crimson smothered the crisp white of her gown.

Her body started to shake. She grabbed the post of her bed to keep her upright. She felt cold, and a loud roaring entered her ears. She barely heard Killian saying her name. Aoife looked him in the eye, swallowing the fear that rose in her throat like bile.

"Princess are you alright?"

Nodding, "yes, just go after that man. Please, find him."

He took in her unkempt appearance, his eye widening at the blood that covered her. He stepped toward her his hand reaching up as if to touch her.

"What happened here?" a deep voice growled. Aoife glanced at the doorway as Killian's body went rigid.

Liam.

Aoife thought she would cry from relief.

"I heard a disturbance coming from inside the room. A man was trying to kidnap the princess," Killian bowed.

Kidnap? He was trying to throw me from the window. Aoife thought as she slid to the floor. The post of her bed digging into her back, she held her throbbing ribs.

Liam's jaw looked so tight she thought that it would snap from the pressure it was under. Liam's blue eyes pierced Aoife, she closed her eyes and concentrated on breathing. A storm rumbled inside him.

"Search the forest. Gather a few more men, tell them that you are looking for a man who tried to enter the palace." His voice was as thunder clapping in the sky. "*Now* Killian."

A dark looked passed over the man's face as he left the room. Liam crossed to Aoife and knelt beside her. He reached out and held her upright as he looked at her. His eyes seemed to clash, like lightning in a storm.

"Malcolm" Liam called. A large figure filled her doorway, her shadows emerging from the dark into the light. "Go wake the king- "

"NO! No, he must not be told," she gripped his arm tightly. Alarm gripping at her heart as she clung to his sleeve with one arm. The movement caused her ribs to protest in pain.

"Aoife..." his tone had finality to it.

"Liam, please do not. For my own reasons we cannot tell him. I cannot tell him. Not yet." Her eyes filled with desperate tears, she matched his intensity with her own. If her father knew, her freedom would be limited to just the stone walls. She would be banned from the woods. Trapped like a bird in a cage.

He leaned his head closer to hers, his forehead inches away from hers. His breath blew her face, she shivered.

"Another secret to keep?" he whispered under his breath.

Gripping him tighter, she whispered back "yes Liam, just one more secret."

A light of understanding sparked in his sky-blue eyes.

"Malcolm go to the village and retrieve Maeve for Aoife. Be subtle."

"Liam, she does not need to be summoned at this hour. I will be- "

"Do *not* say fine. Do not lie, I can feel you trembling. And as I cannot stay in your room all night, since you are betrothed, Malcolm will fetch Maeve and bring her here."

He leaned closer to her again, his forehead now resting on hers "for me you will do this, I have two secrets of yours and you owe me."

She closed her eyes and nodded, consenting to his demands. *How did the man know where to find her?* She looked at the door to tell Malcolm where Maeve's house was, but he was already gone, she hadn't even heard him leave.

Liam smelled of damp wood as if he had been outside in the rain. His blue eyes were impossibly bright against the dim fire. He was staring at her, his jaw still tight, the muscle jumping. Aoife's face flooded with heat when she realized how close she was to Liam.

She realized her hand was still gripping his arm, and she slowly let go so he wouldn't notice her retreating. A scarlet handprint was painted on his sleeve. Aoife gasped and looked at her hands.

"I am so sorry," she tried backed away horrified. Her ribs screamed in protest.

He watched her closely, as if he was watching a bird trying to escape from a wolf's clutches.

His eyes softened. "Let me help you." He stood and stalked to her bed ripping the sheets into shreds of fabric. There was a tightness to him as he moved. Aoife shifted to her knees, trying to pick up the glass that surrounded her.

"Leave it," Liam sighed, agitation in his voice. He pulled a chair close to the fire, setting the strips he had just ripped from her bed on the floor beside it. He approached her and bent down and picked her up she sucked in breath at the movement in her ribs.

Concern crossed his face.

"My ribs are...uh... sore." Aoife admitted.

He set her softly into the chair near the fire.

"I could have walk," Aoife said, her face flushing.

He ignored her and reached for her hands, his touch felt like a whisper across her skin. His coarse fingers moved quickly to bind her hands, which were trembling slightly. His gentleness was undoing her slightly and tears sprang to the back of her eyes, her throat felt tight. She stared into the fire to dry her eyes, she did not want to cry in front of

Liam, not for anything. She placed a small smile on her face as she watched his hands work swiftly to tie strips of fabric around her ribs.

Aoife cleared her throat. "As far as late evenings go, this actually isn't the worst I've had. Normally my dreams turn to nightmares. It's curious really that I can sleep at all," she said and let out a laugh with madness behind it.

"This is not a joke. Nor a dream, a man attacked-. You should feel safe in your own home. We-" He stopped, exasperated.

She paused before responding, his black hair fell into his face shading his impossibly blue eyes. She wiped at her eyes, as a few tears had escaped after all. He finished bandaging her ribs and stayed where he was. As if he could shield her from the danger. She lightly laid her bandaged hand on his hand that was closest to her lap. She waited until he looked at her.

"Struggling is part of the greatness of a story," she smiled at him and patted his hand, "Nothing happened Liam-"

"Nothing happened? You are covered in scrapes and bruises. For your sake we will not tell the King, but for my sake we will say something did happen! What if someone attempts this again?" His eyes flashed dangerously, his voice the same strained even tone. It scared her more than if he were yelling.

He had voiced her concerns, but that was her burden, not his. She had to admire him for his sense of duty to her. They remained in silence for a long while. She could feel the anger rolling off him.

Someone would attempt this again? She pinched her nose between her fingers. Her shoulders tensed, threats were rolling in like the fog for her kingdom. She laid her head on his shoulder, trying to gain strength from his anger. Liam gently wrapped her in his arms, careful to not put pressure on her ribs. Aoife did not know how long they stayed that way.

"Aoife, I-"

The door slammed open, in the doorway stood Maeve, her brown hair trailing down her back in windswept elegance. She looked furious. Aoife sat up on the chair, her throat felt thick as a little sound of pain escaped her lips. She shot her hand up and smothered her mouth to keep any more sounds from straying. Something in her broke open when she saw Maeve. She felt Liam staring at her, and she thought she could hear his teeth grinding.

Maeve entered the room her hands on her hips, Malcolm entered after her filling the doorframe with his body. He leaned against the wall a grim line set on his face. Maeve walked up to Aoife and studied her cuts, gently picking up her injured hands.

"Why wasn't anyone here protecting her? That is all of your jobs is it not?" The red flecks in her eyes sparked, like flame catching on wood, threatening to burn it to ash.

Maeve was like the waves crashing on the sea, always moving and changing. Powerful and sure. Aoife wished she could have some of her strength.

"I need you to calm down, Maeve. We weren't in the room with her. Nobody heard what was going on-" Malcolm said.

She rounded on Malcolm, her mouth curling viciously. He held his ground, Aoife noticed his eyes widen in surprise at the ferocity of her friend.

"When there is silence there is not much that can be done. Guards were only alerted because Aoife kicked glass onto the floor. We would not purposely be careless with her life." he defended.

"Well someone was! Look at her Malcolm, she is *bleeding*. She was hurt." Their eyes collided, Aoife thought she could see animals snapping at each other the way they looked at one another.

Liam stood, his whole frame seemed to be racked with fury and disappointment. Aoife couldn't understand the latter of the two emotions. He set the glass he was holding in what was the rest of her torn sheets. He shifted toward Aoife almost instinctively, as if to protect her from Maeve and Malcolm who were about to rip each other open.

Liam smelt of damp wood and pine, her heart relaxed in her chest. He brought familiarity to her, the forest was her true home. She could breath. She took strength from the familiar smells, and from having Maeve here with her.

"Maeve," Aoife whispered, fear clung to her like a frightened child gripping its mother. She knew she was close to crying.

Maeve turned to face Aoife and looked suspiciously at Liam. Gauging his proximity to Aoife.

"Out!" She barked. "Both of you, leave," as if it was a second thought she added with a sickening sweet tone, "Malcolm do not ever tell me to calm down again." She turned back around to face her friend.

Malcolm started to back into the shadows of the hallway, hands raised in surrender.

Liam shifted closer to Aoife. Maeve's eye narrowed as her eyes flicked between the two. She sighed deeply as if she had lived for many years.

"Liam, I need to help stop the bleeding. I need to see what else needs mending, for modesty's sake, you must leave."

Liam glanced at Aoife as if to get her permission. She nodded, but hurriedly grabbed his arm before her could step away.

"Remember your promise to me Liam. He can't know. Don't allow anyone to say anything." She was thinking of Killian and the few others helping him. It was big secret, but the stakes were too high. If the king got word, he would confine her to the castle forever. She would have no freedom and would be monitored even more closely. She had already lost so much with her mother's death, she would not lose her ability to leave the confines of the castle's walls.

Please understand me, she prayed in her heart. Her body ached dully, weariness laid across her bones like snow on the branches of trees, creaking under of the weight. There was silence and Aoife felt the air stir around her as Liam walked away, sending another waft of forest to her. She heard the door shut, with the click of the door, Aoife let go and sobbed. Maeve rushed to her and held her.

"Shh you are safe. Shh," her friend comforted. Maeve helped her to be closer to the fire and its warmth. She then moved to the door and commanded Malcolm to fetch a pail of water and for Liam to keep the servants from entering the room.

Maeve worked to clean Aoife's wounds and got her dressed into a new gown. A gown for the day, as the sun was starting to rise. Aoife let her sobs subside. Shutting off her fear from her heart.

Aoife realized how naive she had been, thinking that she was safe in her castle walls. The intruder had come to her, he had known where she slept. Nowhere was safe, and tonight showed Aoife that she could not rely on anyone to protect her.

She would not let this happen again. She would protect herself at all costs.

What big ears you have.

The better to *hear* you with my dear.

Chapter 11

Aoife spent the rest of the night in a thoughtless stupor. She watched as Maeve burned her clothes and scrubbed all blood from the room. Maeve had re-wrapped Aoife's ribs to control the movement. Aoife didn't move from the chair, her body throbbed at the thought of moving.

"How will we explain all this?" Maeve asked.

Without removing her lifeless eyes from the fire Aoife responded, "I had a nightmare and, in my fright, knocked into my shelf causing my injury."

"No one will believe-"

"We will need to make them believe Maeve. I am not hiding this because I am brave."

"Aoife what are you saying?" Maeve came closer to Aoife, kneeling at her feet.

"I am a coward. If my-" she stopped, not wanting to involve anyone in her deepest thoughts about her father. Maeve had always known of the tension between Aoife and the King. But this was a something that needed to be locked away.

At least I make a good queen of secrets.

"Don't mind me Maeve, I am just in shock." Aoife smiled to reassure her friend.

Maeve didn't look convinced, sighing deeply she went to the wardrobe and pulled out a warm dress for Aoife to wear. She helped her put it on. Aoife could see that Maeve struggled to hold back her thoughts, she was grateful her friend held her tongue. She needed a minute longer to sort through her thoughts.

Maeve opened her mouth to speak and was cut off by Neasa who sashayed through the door.

"Wake up princess..." her shrill voice faded into silence, which grated on Aoife's nerves. "Maeve what are you doing here? Princess! Wha-what happened to you?!" The plump woman's eyes filled with tears, she rushed to the princess, her hands gently holding the bandaged remains of Aoife's hands.

Aoife forced a giggle, "Neasa you will never guess what a child I am. I had a frightful dream and fell off my bed, knocking my table down with me. Which of course had my pitcher on it. Well I fell into the glass! Can you believe my folly? Lucky for me Maeve came this morning earlier than usual."

Neasa's mouth parted like a fish, she looked at Maeve for confirmation.

"You know the princess' overactive imagination," she smiled sweetly, shrugging her shoulders.

Aoife was hoping that if she could convince Neasa, the whole castle wouldn't think anything of it. She would just look like a silly girl, dreaming silly dreams.

Neasa laughed heartily, "Oh my dear! What shall I do with you?"

Gossip, like you do best. "Help me clean up my mess?" She looked at her nurse sheepishly. The emotion pounded against her ribs, deception never sat right with Aoife.

Neasa clicked her tongue, "I will finish tidying the room, you go on to your lessons. Rowan does not like waiting."

"You are right about that," Maeve laughed. Maeve linked arms with Aoife to hide the fact that Aoife couldn't get up by herself. The two girls left quickly, shutting the motherly woman in with Aoife's nightmare.

To her surprise Liam and Malcolm were both waiting for them outside the door.

"I thought I told you two to keep people from entering the room?" Maeve raised her hand to her hip, keeping her other arm linked with Aoife's. Frustration was written over her face.

"You try keeping that women out of Aoife's room. Even I wouldn't dare pick a fight with a mother." Malcolm retorted, putting his hands-on hips, mimicking Maeve.

Aoife didn't hear Maeve's response; her eyes had locked on Liam. She watched as he came forward and took her other arm, allowing her more stability.

"You should be resting." His voice was tight.

She coughed, ignoring Liam and interrupting Maeve and Malcolm, who were still going around in the same argument.

"We should all be clear about what happened tonight. In case anyone asks. I decided... Um, well, the story is..." She felt like a fool.

Maeve, with irritation, filled in the men about Aoife's chosen explanation. As well as, adding her own opinion on the matter. Aoife shivered as she watched Maeve explain the story, the fairy-looking girl kept her hand on her hip in severe displeasure. Liam watched Aoife, she smiled at him to reassure him that she was fine. His mouth turned down in response.

"Aoife, I think you should move rooms," Maeve said, turning her full attention on her friend. She looked exhausted and a stab of guilt hit Aoife. She should have been able to sleep. Aoife wondered if she looked the same way.

"And what would the king think? I have been in that room since I was born."

"Tell the king you feel like change before your wedding…" Maeve's voice died off in uncertainty.

The King would demand a better answer than that if his only daughter has a whim to move. Maeve knew this as well as Aoife.

Aoife smiled at her friend, her heart thumped loud inside her rib cage, fear racing through her body. If the king suspected anything, all freedom would be lost. Until she was married off, but she still had no idea what the character of her husband would be. The truth was that Aoife did not want to move any closer to the King and his watchful eye. Before she could answer Malcolm stepped closer to her, his face serious.

"He might not try anything of this nature again so soon after his failure," Malcolm said.

Was he trying to comfort Maeve?

Aoife watched Maeve as she stared Malcolm down, doubt and hope fought for control on her face.

"We will strengthen the guards around the area, especially at night. We will protect her better," Malcolm shrugged.

"Do not shrug at this," Maeve hissed, "her life is not to be treated as nothing more than a shrug. I will hold you personally responsible if anything happens to her. The king would not be pleased either, but my wrath is the one you should fear."

Liam moved closer to Aoife, their bodies were almost touching. Her face warmed as well.

"Shh Maeve, remember Neasa," Aoife nodded toward the door. She stepped out of the reach of both Maeve and Liam, facing all three.

Liam spoke with a finality, "This will not happen to the princess again. I give my word."

"I need all your words. This does not get back to anyone, not the king. Nor your prince." She looked at Liam. He seemed to flinch at the last word. Her face flushed. "It seems we are all in agreement that last night will not be repeated."

More servants seemed to start crawling into the hallways. Aoife motioned them forward. She held her side as they walked down the corridors. Her breathing was coming out in shallow gasps. She tried to draw little attention herself. She dropped slowly behind the rest of the group.

Malcolm and Maeve seemed to be arguing again. Aoife wondered in Malcolm was trying anything to get the tension to go out of Maeve. Aoife hoped he succeeded. Aoife grabbed the wall with one hand, she started to feel dizzy. A warm hand slipped around her waist.

Aoife blushed to see that the arm belonged to Liam. His face was masked with concern and anger.

"Are you alright?" The roughness to his voice nearly undid the emotions she was trying to desperately keep locked up inside her. She nodded, clenching her teeth.

She wanted to yell that she was not alright, that for a long time it seemed that she had not been alright. Aoife was afraid to let herself free the pain that ran inside her, in case it broke her. Aoife groaned on the inside, she was tired of pitying herself. She distracted her thoughts by counting her steps.

Liam kept his arm around her until they reached the doors of Rowan's quarters. Maeve went in without looking back. Aoife could hear Rowan's booming voice fill the room.

"Aoife, I will be here waiting. I am not leaving," Liam said, gave her elbow a soft squeeze and melted into the shadows of the hall. Aoife held her chin higher as she walked into the room, her heart pounding in her chest.

***

The next few days passed by in a blur, Maeve and Liam had refused to leave Aoife alone at all. Liam had kept true to his word. Only Malcolm and Liam switched off watching her now. Killian, according to

Malcolm was no longer trusted to watch over her. She knew they were stretching themselves too thin, but she never heard them complain.

Malcolm brought a lightness to the atmosphere. He spent most of his time flirting with Maeve. It irritated her to no end, but Aoife could see that Malcolm was trying to distract her. Aoife was grateful to Malcolm. Since that night Maeve and Liam seemed to blame themselves for not saving Aoife. She wanted them to release that guilt. She thought Malcolm was very good at distraction.

Liam hovered, but whenever he left to train the men, Aoife felt vulnerable. As if she were walking around with a target pinned to her head, and she just had to wait for the arrow to fly.

Maeve still thought that it was best for Aoife to move from her room. Maeve insisted while Aoife persisted. They settled on an agreement: Aoife would leave her door open at night, so anything could be heard inside her room. When Aoife tried to disagree, arguing that it wouldn't be proper because of the guards.

Malcolm hastily agreed with Maeve, "Will just be between Liam and I. No other lads will be watching over you."

Aoife glared at Malcolm, calling him a traitor. She wanted to keep resisting, because that meant that none of the incident happened. Aoife could pretend it was a dream, she could believe her own lie. Maeve and Liam would not let her keep it as an imaginary thought.

Her room, which once felt safe, now felt uncertain and cold.

Night is when the terrors would crawl into her mind, often she would wake drenched in sweat. Normally she wouldn't be able to sleep after that, she would lay awake and wait for morning's light to rupture the darkness around her.

One night after waking again from a nightmare she started to cry. Exhaustion filled her body. She flipped her face into her pillow, allowing herself this moment of weakness.

A light knock sounded on the door, Aoife snapped her head up to look, Liam filled the door frame, his shoulders tense.

"Liam... I-" She quickly wiped at her face, removing the tears roughly.

"May I come in?"

Without her consent and ignoring the fact that she was engaged to another man and all other social propriety, he crossed the room until her was sitting on the bed next to her. She raised the quilt higher to her chin, in the recesses of her mind she knew that the king would not be happy with this exchange. Nor would her betrothed. Doubt overwhelmed her she was about to send him away when he started to hum.

"What are you doing?" She asked.

He put a finger to his lips and motioned for her to lie down. She sat rigid in the bed, pulling again at the blanket. Though he was hidden in the colors of the night she could feel his gaze.

He made his way to the fire and stroked it and sat down on the chair that was placed there. Her eyes adjusted to the dark where she could make out his form, he was leaning forward towards her. His humming seemed to be ending.

"Where is Malcolm?" She tried again.

"Sleeping, as you should be." Silence. "Did you know you make no sounds when you sleep. As if death curls around you in your sleep. Odd."

Aoife cringed at the description, "I beg your pardon?"

"Except when you wake up, then you make a lot of noise. In fact, I think it is the most I ever hear from you."

Aoife laughed, "I speak when I must, I never have much to say."

"Or maybe others have too much to say."

She pursed her lips feeling defensive of her people. "I have a lot to learn, so it benefits me to know the wisdom of others, don't you think?"

"You should be careful who you take advice from. You are born to rule, not to be ruled." He responded, his voice was so soft it seemed to blend in with the night.

"Isn't it the duty of a ruler to listen to the needs of the subjects? I don't know everything."

"That will be true, but not everyone has advice worth heeding. Experience is a teacher as well. Trust your own mind. The people will only see one side, it is your job to see all sides, and new sides."

Aoife's brow furrowed. *New sides? How was she to do that when she too could be limited in her view?* She looked over at his shape in the dark. *Was ruling men in battle the same as ruling a kingdom in peace?* Her mind began to spin with the ideas he presented her. She wasn't aware how long she had been silent.

"Spoken like a true leader," she said awkwardly. Hoping that he hadn't noticed her pause, Rowan hated when she lost focus. She thought she heard Liam scoff.

"Give yourself time, you will learn it."

Aoife was grateful for the darkness to cover the heat that rose to her face. Her heart thumped against her chest, but she wasn't afraid. She felt the weight of her calling heavy on her shoulders. Maybe therefore the king needed her to be married off, he didn't think she was up to the task.

Would her husband lead with wisdom? She didn't know what she would do if she married a cruel man. Or a fool for that matter, but one could work with a fool.

"Liam tell me, what is your prince like? Is he a kind? A good leader? Wise? Strong? Smart?"

A thousand questions rushed through her mind. She had to bite down on her tongue, so as not to overwhelm herself. Her questions were met with stillness. She leaned forward wondering if he had fallen asleep.

"Liam?" She shifted again on her bed and leaned her head back against the wall.

"Would you like to hear a story?" he answered roughly.

If Liam was changing the subject the prince must be horrible. Aoife sighed deeply her ribs groaned. She sucked in sharply and held her ribs tight.

"I do love stories."

When he spoke next it was in a language Aoife had never heard before. It sounded like a song as he spoke, she knew nothing of what he said, but the soft and rough tones weaved together. She closed her eyes to see what the words drew in her mind, her body and mind relaxed.

Aoife wondered why Liam, a man she knew for a few weeks could make her feel safe. It bothered her, she didn't like to depend on people. And yet within this short time Liam had become a friend and a keeper of her secrets. Yet he held himself back, she knew nothing of his past, only what she had seen was evidence to who he was. Perhaps that was enough, who people truly are always shine through their actions, not the words they speak.

No matter how she trusted him the truth gnawed in her heart. He would not always be there for her, she needed to learn how protect herself. But how? Who would dare teach a princess how to fight for herself?

Aoife fell asleep to the soothing voice that weaved a story around her.

Chapter 12

"Are you listening to me Princess?" Rowan's gruff voice startled her.

"I am sorry Rowan. my mind was... far away. Forgive me."

He exhaled heavily and threw up his hands. "When are you going to learn to listen girl? I am here to help you become a proper Queen! If you can't focus long enough on me, how are you going to run a kingdom? How will you be able to protect and serve your people if you are not taking this seriously?"

Her cheeks began to flame, as anger and guilt washed over her. Why did he always doubt her? She bit her lower lip to keep from saying all that entered her mind. She couldn't afford to offend the old grump and gain the king's reproach. Aoife looked over to Maeve's empty seat, she had not come today. Loneliness settled around her, like an arm around a friend. Aoife was starting to resent that Maeve's father needed her to bring in the harvest.

The wind rushing through the trees drew her attention, the docile green leaves were now all consumed by the red and orange of autumn. It looked as if fire was absorbing all the life from the tree, creating beauty from the reminder of death.

A desperate wave washed over her to retreat into the woods. However, she knew that Rowan was right, if she was to become a useful queen she needed to listen to what the bard had to say.

"I am sorry Rowan. I am focused now-"

A knock sounded at the door, a young man entered the room facing Rowan. "King Eamonn sends for you Rowan."

The old bard rubbed his hands over his face. He seemed to age before Aoife's eyes. He mumbled to himself, something about needy royals. He stalked over to his shelf and retrieved a large volume and shoved the book in Aoife's hands.

"Since you are fond of reading and wandering around in that head of yours, read this. It is the history of this people, all the tribes and kingdoms and how they came to be. I will see you next in three days' time. If you have it finished I will resume teaching, you. If not, do not bother coming to see me."

He stalked out of the room, the boy on his heels.

Aoife set the book on the table and went to lean out the window, it was still early in the day, dark clouds threatened on the horizon.

She could faintly hear the ringing of swords coming from the direction of the courtyard. An idea formed at the back of her mind. She seized the book off the table and hurried into the corridor. Killian peeled himself off the wall and glanced at her with boredom.

"Are your lessons done for the day?"

"What are you doing here?"

Killian scowled. "Disappointed?"

"No, I'm sorry Killian, it just has been awhile…" She faded off, she was in fact disappointed she hoped the Liam would have been there.

"Are you done with your lessons?"

"Y-actually no, Rowan was called away by King Eamonn, but he was going to show me the armory and the training that is happening by your men. He insisted that I see it today. All apart of bettering our kingdom," she was rambling. "Would you mind taking me Killian?"

"Are you sure you would not rather spend your time on something else? Like reading that large book in your hands? After all, nothing special ever happens there. Just a lot of sweaty boys trying to be men," Killian eyes flashed with humor, his smile was sharp, showing all his teeth.

She shivered, Killian always had such strong opinions. None of which Aoife ever agreed with.

"I am sure. Take me there again," she raised her chin.

He shrugged and pivoted on his foot walking down the corridor, he didn't pause or look back to see if she followed him. If he would have looked back, he would have seen the biggest smile planted on Aoife's face. She couldn't shake the excitement that ran along her spine, something was about to change.

***

Killian was right, the armory stunk of unbathed men, despite the armory leading to outside the stench made Aoife's eyes sting. She made a mental note to have the place thoroughly scrubbed.

All sort of trinkets lined the walls. They seemed to wink at Aoife with deadly gleam. Armor shells were placed carelessly on shelves

"I did not realize all the different ways a man could die hung on these palace walls," she whispered more to herself than anyone.

Killian looked thoughtfully at her. "Well princess, every man has different skills and limitations. We like to have our options. We search for a weapon that fits our...taste."

"Are you telling me that every weapon is unique to every man?'

"Aye, the weapon is the power of the man. And the greater power is dependent on the skill of the man holding the weapon."

"Is that all that is important to the fight? Power over someone else?"

Killian raised in eyebrow, boredom covering his face.

"Shall we continue then Princess?" Killian ignored the question.

They walked in silence through a narrow passageway. The walls were cold and damp. It seeped into Aoife's bones. They walked on in silence, there was a narrow strip of light that flooded into the hall from the open door of the courtyard. The clashing of swords clapped loudly through the tunnel.

They emerged on the other side, Killian glancing back to check if she was behind him. She blinked hard against the natural light. They tucked themselves away in the corner of the courtyard so as not to be a distraction.

Just as before Liam stood at the front of his men. His black hair tied behind his neck in a knot. His eyes flashed as he yelled out orders. His eyes roaming over his men, never missing anything. Every misstep was called to attention. He was never harsh, only firm.

Aoife wondered if he had always been so observant. She wondered what would have happened to him if he made a mistake. Her mouth turned up slightly at the thought.

"How long do they practice?" Aoife whispered. She glanced at the man next to her, his mouth was turned down and his gray eyes watched the movement in front of him. The movements were hypnotic in a way, but the way he watched it unsettled Aoife. It was as if he enjoyed the brutality.

He answered curtly, "Four hours, enough for each man to train before or after their rotations."

"That is a long time, do they not tire?"

He laughed humorously, "Truthfully they should train harder and longer. Liam is too soft, giving them rest. In a battle, fighting goes on for hours. You need stamina to keep going. If you get tired, you lose ground, or your life."

Aoife had never thought of that before. There were many things she had never considered before the warrior of Laoch came. Somehow, the unimaginable seemed possible.

Killian continued. "Liam isn't working with much; these men will never fight like the warriors of Laoch. Yet Liam insists on doing his duty. That's all he ever does." His lip curled into a cruel smile, his eyes hardened as kept he kept his eyes on the attention.

Killian's superior attitude grated on Aoife's already raw nerves. These were men were her people. They protected those who could not protect themselves.

"We might not be much in numbers, but we know what we fight for. And *that* is the real stamina, the reasons behind the fight. You can always go on if there is too much to lose."

She saw Killian turn his head to her lazily, as if she were a pesky fly that was just making noise, flying around his head. Irritation bubbled in her veins, she put a hand over her mouth to keep her from saying speaking and turned her eyes on Liam watching as he corrected a young soldier.

She wanted to show Killian that her men were fighters. Before she could think of consequences, swallowing the fear that was rising in her throat like bile. She held her head high and placed smile on her face. She hoped no one noticed her trembling hands. She walked toward Liam, her smile growing with her nervousness. She could hear the roar of clanging metal fade into silence. The men's whispers became louder like a swarm of bees as she neared the front of the room.

Liam walked toward her his face calm, except for the worry that pooled in his eyes.

"Princess Aoife what a surprise."

"I wanted to see how the men were coming along. And commend them for doing a good job. I am sure it is not easy." The men chuckled. Aoife's face warmed as she realized the men were listening to her every word. She stood straighter and her smile increased. She clasped her hands together willing them to be still. Looking desperately at Liam, an amused grin covered his face.

He pointed to the men with his chin. Telling her to look away from him. Nodding his head, he faced his men, giving her no choice but to face them.

She continued, "It is worth it to us, to all of us. Our land and people are worth protecting. You will do us all proud." Curling one of her hands into a fist she placed it over heart as she has seen Liam do.

To her surprise the men raised their hands to their hearts. Her hands stopped shaking. She looked over to Liam, he had faced her and placed his hand on his heart, bowing slightly to her. Her heart pounded, curtseying in return.

Liam commanded the men to return to their training. Once again metal scraping on metal filled Aoife's ears.

She turned to leave as he reached out gently on the elbow turning her to face him. "You did well. The lads will be talking about this for days."

"I hope I didn't disrupt anything, that was not my intention. I- well- I needed to…" She trailed off. She looked at Liam who had dark circles under his eyes. She wondered how long it had been since he had gotten a good night sleep. Shame filled her face, if she could just watch over herself she wouldn't need anyone.

"Thank you for last night, I haven't been... sleeping." She looked at him, he was dedicated to his commands, but at what cost? His health? Surely his prince wouldn't want that for his soldiers. "Take care of yourself Liam."

She wished she could say that she would take care of herself. A muscle jumped in his jaw.

"My priority is your protection, whatever form that takes, I am willing."

Hope knocked on her heart with those words. Before she could stop herself, she stepped closer to him, dropping her voice.

"Even if it is unconventional?" Her mind started to rotate. She hoped he would agree.

His eyes narrowed in suspicion. "What ideas are you turning around in there?" he pointed to her head.

She shook her head, wanting to hope for a little longer that her scheme could hatch. That Liam was the man that she thought he was.

"Come to me later, alone. I'll be where you first found me." She said.

She felt his stare on her back as she half ran from the room.

Aoife returned to Rowan's study, grabbed her scarlet cloak and with the book in hand headed out of the castle's walls and into the embrace of the forest. She would go to her mother's place, only where he could find her. She pulled the hood up to hide her face and she avoided people on the way to the woods. No one would know she was missing. As she stepped into the entrance of the woods the weight in her stomach lifted as she put the castle behind her.

She would learn how to fight, and she knew who her teacher was going to be. She needed him to hold one more secret for her.

The man with all her secrets.

Chapter 13

The snapping of a twig broke the revere Aoife's mind had wandered into. She felt the stiff, coldness of her body as she sat against the rough bark of the tree. Rowan's book which she still clutched in her hands, she had covered a small amount of the reading. She shook her head and gently shut the book. She would have to start the book over not remembering a single detail. She groaned, reminded of the task she had to finish it in three days' time.

She looked toward the sound and came to find clear blue eyes staring back to meet her own. Her face burned red and she was grateful for the coolness of autumn that would mask the blush into a symptom of the cold.

"Do you grow books from your fingertips? I seem to find you with a new book every time we speak," Liam said to her, bending down to look her in the eyes.

She laughed and laid her head back against the tree, "Are you implying that I use magic? That could get me in trouble you know. I will soon hear rumors of my being a fairy. And what would your prince say about marrying a fairy woman?" She clicked her tongue shaking her head in mock horror. "No Liam, I am an ordinary woman with the ability to read."

"Sounds like magic to me." He laughed.

She shifted forward, trying to regain feeling in her limbs before standing up. She smiled at Liam as he studied her. A nervous energy began to grow within her as she glanced around wildly for anybody nearby.

Liam smiled lazily.

"What were you doing in the armory with Killian again today?"

"Liam," she said softly, she had to gain some nerve. She breathed deeply, the pain from her ribs had become tolerable. "Liam, I have a question for you." He cocked his head to the side, giving her a half smile. He nodded for her to go on.

"Will you teach me how to fight? How to defend myself?" she couldn't look at him. She let her hair cover her face giving it more shade. She willed herself to be still. And looked him in the eyes, knowing he needed to see her earnest behind her words. That it wasn't a passing want. She needed him to believe her. His eyes widened and then hardened.

"There is no need for you to learn princess. You have guards all around you who can protect you. I will protect you," he retorted.

She swallowed the anxiety and frustration that was starting to build itself inside her. Aoife stared at him, his sea blue eyes much more profound against his pitch-black hair. His jaw was clenched in anger, his body tense in his crouched position next to her by the roots of the trees.

She stood up, needing to be as equal with him as he could. He rose with her, never looking away from her face. She was tall for a woman coming to the top of his shoulders. She had to look up at him.

The trees seemed to move with the tension that rolled off them both.

"Liam, I was alone that night. I got away due to luck only. You weren't there to protect me. You weren't even on guard that night-" she started.

"I will not let that happen again, we are more prepared. I will be on guard," he cut in.

Her shoulders began ache with the tension she was feeling. Like a bottle about to blow under pressure.

"That is just it. You will not always be there. I cannot be monitored all day long! I need to learn to protect myself!" Her voice started to rise. "I don't want to feel fear like that again. I don't want to feel helpless. The only one who can always watch after me, is me!" anger died as the fear grew.

His face was like stone, taking her in, taking in her words, not giving anything in return.

"Please, Liam," she whispered.

A cold breeze danced over her and Liam, bringing her long hair into her face. She breathed deeply and squared her shoulders. Sleepless nights filled with fear is not how she wanted to live. Life was more than that. She couldn't wait around always being protected while others watched after her. She was a good student, though she doubted Rowan would agree, she could learn how to fight.

When she finally met his gaze, she read the frustration echoing in his own eyes to match hers. Her throat ached with unshed tears and unsaid words.

"Your father will not be pleased," he stated.

A flutter of hope ran along her spine. "He always did like surprises."

Liam's mouth pulled down into a deep frown. He arched a brow, most likely debating whether to give in to her. The excitement grew in her chest.

"Father will never know," she rushed on. "We will meet here, just like normal. He won't suspect a thing. I will have to tell Maeve, so she will help cover for us."

His eyes searched hers "I suppose Maeve would not like to be left out of this teaching either?"

Aoife sighed in relief, "I am sure she would love it, she is always up for an adventure. Besides women warriors sounds fierce do they not? A kingdom could stand for a little more of those. This could be evolution."

He didn't look convinced, but his mouth grew to a ghost of a smile. "You are full of new ideas. I wonder what your betrothed will do with such a princess."

Her face flushed, she forgot about her betrothed. He father often told her to reign in her ideas and thinking, that was only after her mother's accident. Father had never been the same after that.

"He or any other prince for that matter would be lucky to marry me."

"Aye," he said softly, he stepped closer to her sizing her up, his grin flashing wickedly. "Tomorrow then we will begin. You must do as I say and take corrections."

She nodded, the fear evaporating.

Chapter 14

The day passed by too slowly. Too excited to sleep, she had spent the night reading the book Rowan gave her willing herself to focus on the words in front of her. The book told that the merging of the tribes and kingdoms was nearly impossible, it always ended with bloodshed and war and more separation of the people. Men seemed to care more for land and riches then for people and their lives. It unsettled her, why would the king suggest an alliance to the prince of Laoch if this was always the outcome? In her mind she only saw the fall of her kingdom.

Liam hold told Aoife that the surrounding tribes were getting more violent as the days had past, but nothing that required a retaliation. The unsettling feeling would not leave her, not even when dawn stretched its rays across the sky.

Aoife set the book aside, hoping that this brutal fate would not meet either kingdom.

"Malcolm?" She called.

He stepped into the room only to lean against the door frame a sly small curled around his lips. "Princess, no sleep for you again?"

She waved her hand to dismiss his concern. "I was reading, Rowan's instructions." He raised an eyebrow. She continued, "Malcolm, I want to inquire after Maeve, will you bring a note to her?"

"No."

"Pardon?"

"I am not a messenger boy. If you need to inquire, inquire yourself. You have not been to town to fetch those dresses. Let us go see her."

Aoife laughed, "Excellent point, however I get the feeling that you are now using me to see Maeve. That wouldn't have anything to do with it now would it?"

He winked at her and Aoife laughed again. Today would be a good day she thought to herself. Besides she had plenty of time to spare before she would have to meet with Liam.

She ordered Malcolm to leave and close the door so that she could prepare herself for town. She dressed herself and sat down at the mirror to braid her hair. She looked closely at her reflection, it looked different somehow. Her blue eyes with specks of gray seemed to sparkle with new life. Her skin was paler, but she would blame lack of sleep for that.

Aoife's heart felt near to bursting from her chest. She remembered feeling this way as a child, and in moments with Maeve. it was happiness. Aoife moved to braid her gold hair and stopped. She dropped her hands and moved toward the door cloak in hand, she decided to let her hair run wild.

Today was full of possibilities.

***

When they reached the village there were more people in the streets selling all manner of trinkets and goods. Aoife loved the smells and the noise that surrounded the happy people, all seemed to pass her by not recognizing her. Malcolm looked relaxed teasing the princess all the way there. More than once Aoife saw his hand hovering by his weapon that hung around his hips.

"Let us stop in the shop first, then I won't have to worry about the time."

"In a great hurry, are you?"

Yes. Aoife was eager to start her lessons with Liam, hoping to get Maeve in time to join them.

Aoife walked into the shop, fabrics lined the walls and the floors. Aoife could hear a muffled voice coming from behind the counter. When the girl realized she was there she gasped in surprise.

"Princess! So, you are back then? I was worried I cut all them measurements for nothing," the girl smiled warmly at her. "Let me just fetch them for you."

"Do you mind wrapping them? I don't want it to get ruined."

"Of course, Princess! Right away!"

The woman set to work, moving quickly to finish the job. Aoife looked around the store, while, Malcolm kept outside.

"I was wondering if you knew anyone in the village who would be reliable to deliver these packages to the castle? I am not yet finished with my business in town, but they do need to start working on them, or their dresses will never be finished in time."

The woman rubbed her chin with her hand, muttering something to herself. "My brother could do it princess."

"He is reliable?"

"Aye princess, a good solid lad. He will get the job done."

Aoife nodded her head, her eye caught on silver chain with a pouch hanging from the side. Aoife picked it up, looking at it from all sides.

"That is for around the waist your highness. Easier to carry your items."

"I have never seen anything like this before."

The girl smiled and blushed, "I was...uh.. experimenting."

"Are you selling it?"

"Are you offering?" She squeaked.

Aoife giggled at the shock on the shopkeeper's face. "I am, I will also take that cloak you have behind you. The color is beautiful, and I know just who it would be perfect for. That is if it is not already sold?"

The girls mouth opened and closed in disbelief, no doubt tonight she and her brother would go home wealthier than they thought they would. The cloak was a deep purple, the color of a plum with silver thread embroidered on the edges.

Aoife left the shop with two parcels in her hand, leaving a pouch of gold for the girl and her brother for their work.

"Decided to buy yourself a new cloak?" Malcolm gestured to her hands.

"I could never part with my red cloak for all the world! No, this one is for Maeve, she deserves something for herself."

They wove between the houses until they reached Maeve's. Aoife could see only men in the field, she knocked on her door and a small girl opened it. She called for Maeve, staring at Aoife with wonder filled eyes.

Maeve came out, her dark brown hair tied in a braid behind her was falling out and flour was on her cheek.

"Aoife! What are you doing here?" The girl looked relieved as she stepped outside to hug her friend.

"I wanted to see you, I have something I need to tell you, in private."

"Well you heard her Malcolm, shoo," she waved her hand as if waving away pest.

Aoife supposed that he already knew, or she did not care if he knew. He could help Liam hide this secret.

He smirked at, "I already know, so really I have a right to be here, same as you."

Maeve's bemused expression turned wary. They stepped away from her house and further into the field, were they would not be overheard.

"Maeve, Liam has agreed to teach me to fight! He said he would teach you as well if that is something you wanted! Isn't that just perfect?"

"Fight? Like with actual weapons?" Maeve questioned.

"No with your books," Malcolm broke in. "We will teach you to throw them at your enemies until they run away in terror."

"You jest now but let us see how well you hold up under that pressure. In fact, I know the perfect book in my room-" Maeve retorted.

Aoife wanted to give them their moment, but she needed to know if Maeve would come with her. "Maeve, will you join me? It would be in secret of course, King Eamonn would not take to kindly to- well to any of this. But I must try."

"Aoife why are you in such earnest? Liam will watch over you, there is no need for you to learn such violent actions."

Aoife's heart sunk, her stomach churned. "I would not have thought of this route for myself if it was not forced upon me. I am the only one who can protect myself. I want you to have this same power too." Emotion made her throat ache. Maeve and Aoife eyes locked. They seemed to talk without any words. Silence never deterred them from speaking to each other.

"You lasses are strange ones for sure. I feel like I am missing something." Malcolm said.

"I should think you would be used to that feeling." Maeve retorted. "I do want to join you Aoife. But my father has asked that I remain at home until after the festival. I have to help around here." She gestured toward her home. "Besides, the king has asked that I keep my distance, that we both may focus more. I thought he had told you. That is why I have not been coming."

"What about your studies?" Aoife whispered. Pain etched itself on her face. She felt that King Eamonn had betrayed her, that this was the cruelest thing he had done. She didn't understand why it was so easy for Maeve to accept this either. Was Aoife so easy to throw away? She wanted to force a smile, but her heart felt like it breaks from the fear that stirred inside her.

"After the festival I am to learn trade from the healer in town. After that your father has agreed to let me travel around outside the village and to learn and help the tribes in the surrounding areas. This is my dream," her voice was hopeful, but her eyes held concern.

Aoife's heart jumped into her throat. Maeve had been with Aoife from the beginning and though Aoife tried not to add any extra weight to Maeve's load, she realized in that moment that she had always been. Maeve was like a bird about ready to take flight. What right did Aoife have to take that away.

"I am happy for you!" Aoife pulled her friend into another embrace. "You must still visit, or I will plan on getting sick quite often, just so I can see you." Aoife could feel the tears building up in her eyes.

Maeve's face was soft with concern, she leaned in close, blocking Malcolm from hearing her words. "I will never be to far away Aoife, we are family after all. If you ever need me, I will be there. Besides this is not goodbye, not truly. I will come to you before the festival is over."

I need you now, she thought. A storm of conflict brewed deep inside her heart.

"I must go now, mother will be needing me to get back," Maeve sounded reluctant.

Aoife smiled sincerely at her friend, holding out the packages to her, "Here, these are for you. Think of it as me wishing you luck." Aoife wanted to say more, but words had never been a strength for her, especially when it came to telling what was in her heart.

A mixture of grief and pride settled itself upon her shoulders and burrowed deep within her heart.

"Thank you," Maeve's eyes widened in delight.

"I thought maybe you would need a place to put your herbs," She shrugged her shoulders.

Maeve gripped her arm to comfort. She turned to go and pivoted back around to face Aoife.

"I know you will be a great queen and defender of the people. I have seen it. Believe in yourself Aoife, I believe in you," she held her gaze for a moment longer and turned back to go to her house.

It wasn't until Maeve shut the door that Aoife let the tears fall.

Chapter 15

Aoife paced back and forth waiting for him to arrive. Perhaps he did not know where to meet her. But her found her in her mother's place before…

Liam formed into life from out of the shadows. Aoife jumped back and gasped.

"By the moon! You frightened me. Have you always been able to walk so quietly?"

His eyes sparkled with humor. "Perhaps." He looked over her carefully, observing everything. His brow furrowed.

"You look ill? Are you feeling alright?"

"I am well enough."

"Is it Maeve?"

"Umm..yes," she cleared her throat, biting her lip. She hated that he could see her so clearly. To most people she was able to cover herself, like a pond with pebbles being thrown in the water. Liam looked through the ripples into her reflection.

Frustration flashed through his eyes like lightning across stormy skies.

"All will right itself soon enough," he offered.

His confidence confused Aoife.

He reached for a bundle that was on his back. Aoife wondered why she was so dense as not to see such bulk that he had carried with seeming ease. He laid it out gently, and waved her over to the display of weapons, watching her as she neared him.

"Hold this," he shoved a short handled, thick blade into her hand, she almost dropped it. Gasping, she wondered how men could carry them with such ease!

He retrieved it, replacing it with a new one. This blade was half the height of Aoife, but it was considerably less in weight than the other. Liam nodded to himself, as if he were confirming what he already knew.

"How does this feel in your hand?" He asked.

"Fine, I think. I don't have anything to compare it with."

He reached out for her hand, "May I?"

Aoife didn't understand what he was asking, she warily nodded her head. Liam gently turned her hand over to view her grip with the sword. Her knuckles had gone white from holding it so tight.

Liam's fingers tapped her own, *what was that supposed to mean*? She looked up at him with confusion.

"Loosen your hold, tight enough that it won't be knocked from your hands. Loose enough that you allow for flexibility," he instructed.

Intriguing. She thought to herself. He spoke with command, but it did not agitate her the way instruction from Rowan usually did. She did not just think it was because of the debt she was in to him. It was the manner in which he spoke. It eerily reminded her of the way a king might speak; authority laced with mercy. No wonder the men loved him. He inspired loyalty from the first interaction. It was the way King Eamonn spoke to his people. She felt her mouth twitch and lifted her arm as advised.

"The sword is an extension of you now. You must learn to control the weapon, or you will hurt yourself. This weapon is yours now, no one else will wield it. However, I will hold onto to it for you, until your training is over. Understood?"

Her brow wrinkled. "It is mine? I can't take this; won't someone know that it is missing?"

"All your father's weapons are where they should be. This was my first blade, it is yours now."

"Why would you give it to me?" she said, still confused.

Liam laughed sarcastically. "Are we going to stand here all-day squawking like crows?"

She shook her head. Liam began to teach her proper stance. Where to hold your weight, how to hold the blade. Within the first thirty minutes Aoife was breathing hard and her muscles shook. It took everything she had not to give in to dropping the blade below her chest. This was harder than she thought it was going to be. Liam calmly continued to give her instructions.

It was not until the sun went down that Liam allowed her to drop her weapon. Sweat dripped down her entire body. She panted, trying to gain some air that she had lost. Her body was screaming at her, her ribs being the loudest protesters.

Liam looked on in his usual careful manner. She was grateful that he did not laugh at her.

"Same time tomorrow," Liam took the sword from her. His face, other than hints of amusement, told her nothing of her skill.

He placed the sword back in its wrapping with the other tools and carefully laid them under one tree that refused to be planted on the ground, creating a cubby for hiding things. Covering it with leaves so to any passerby it looked like any other part of the forest.

When Aoife was able to breathe easy again she and Liam made the trek back to the castle. Liam kept his thoughts to himself. Aoife could feel herself grinning at her like a fool. She was sore all over and yet the grin only continued to grow on her face. Like spilled milk on a dress, it was a gradual expansion.

Not only was Liam keeping her secrets, but he was helping her to become something more than she could have imagined for herself. She laughed inwardly at the thought of the Kings and her betrothed face at her yielding a sword.

She would become a capable queen yet, one that both her parents could be proud of. She would be an equal to her husband. Life always carried good and bad. Aoife was excited at the growth she was making personally and wanted to share in that growth with Maeve.

As Aoife crawled into bed that night she let the tears silently fall for the absence of Maeve. And the betrayal of her father for taking her friend away.

***

Aoife was awoken to someone shaking her body. She had to bite the inside of her cheek to stop from protesting from the soreness of her body.

"Princess, your father wishes for you to join him! Princess please get up! We can't keep the king waiting," Neasa moved about her room in a flurry.

"Alright Neasa I'm going."

She carefully rose from her bed, stiffness in every movement. The pain was a reminder that yesterday was no dream. She shuffled to her dresser and quickly put on a plain blue frock. The king once complimented her while she wore it and it so shocked her that anytime she wanted to please her father she would put it on.

"Did the girls receive their fabric Neasa?"

"Oh, they did princess! They were all so excited hardly any of them slept last night. That was all the conversation was about in the servant's hall. They all have many plans of how each dress will be different from each other, they are all determined not to look the same," she smiled tenderly at Aoife. Motherly.

Aoife, "Oh I should have bought one more color. I just didn't know what the girls-"

"Think no more on it, no one is complaining. Tis' like another competition for the festival for them," Neasa nodded as if that was the final word on the whole conversation.

Neasa moved to make the bed when she turned suddenly and held up a book.

"What is this?"

Aoife turned around, tying her hair into a braid. Her brow furrowed. It was something that Aoife had never seen before. She shook her head in confusion.

"I could not tell you nurse. It is not mine," she turned away undisturbed by the presence of another book in her room. For all she knew Rowan had sent it to her to read one more thing. "Where is the king?"

She gracefully rose from her chair. She murmured a goodbye to her nurse and went into the hall, Malcolm waited for her. She noticed that he looked tired as well. No one seemed to be getting sleep anymore. For a second she thought she was keeping him up, then she thought better of it. Malcolm was her friend, but it would not be her disturbing his sleep. She tried twice to start a conversation with him. He seemed too distracted. The echoes of their footsteps were the only thing she heard, Aoife shivered at the loneliness of the sound.

The closer to the King's chamber she got, the more it sounded like a beehive. Servants passed her, nodding their only acknowledgement. She smiled at them as they passed her, but her pulse quickened when she saw her father on his throne. He seemed to her a lot smaller in the chair then he ever had before. Aoife didn't know if that was because she was getting bigger or if he was getting smaller.

He sat straight up, his eyes looking down on the flurry of people around him. His shoulders were slightly drooped, as if stones had been placed on his shoulders. When he finally saw her, she smiled warmly at him, but his face was as immovable as stone.

She bowed to him and he impatiently waved her forward. Standing with his arms behind his back as she approached him.

"Daughter, there are changes that will be made. I expect you to follow them," his brow furrowed, it was in that moment that Aoife noticed his age, how old he really looked. Sorrow was drowning him, and Aoife wondered if he would ever be happy again. If she would ever be able to make him happy.

"It has come to my attention that there has been rumors of rebellions around the kingdom, from neighboring tribes. These men are dangerous, so as a precaution I have sent Rowan to them to see what he can find out. Even those savages know not to touch a learned man."

"How long will he be gone?"

"Your studies are cancelled, I see no point in furthering your education. Besides your husband might not be as indulgent as I have been in allowing you to have so many books."

Her mouth parted in surprise, surely Liam and Malcolm would have warned her, wouldn't they?

"Is that why you sent Maeve away?" hurt bled into her voice.

King Eamonn glared at his daughter. "You do not understand everything yet. Trust that I know more then you and trust my decisions."

"How can I trust you father? You have kept me at a distance, in the dark for so long. You expect me to be a great ruler but tell me nothing. I cannot become a queen blindly. Father if you just-"

"You are fragile and would not understand. Those other tribes would do anything for our wealth and our kingdom! Men want the power of this kingdom and would stop at nothing to get it. Through you and people you associate with. It is too risky," his voice had a finality to it.

Aoife did not want Maeve to suffer for Aoife's ignorance.

"Help me to understand father, I am no longer a child. What if Maeve had an escort then she would not be in danger and-"

"You are more important my dear. I cannot spare a man on her, when there is you. I can't lose- I can't lose to those men, not again."

"I will not suffer the same fate as mother. You must allow me to live my life. Mother would not want us to live this way. Hiding behind our walls in fear. Father please-"

"Enough! Hold your tongue," he said bitterly, "you will do as I bid you, you are my daughter. Until you are married you must do as I say. You're excused."

King Eamonn turned away from her walking from the room. In that moment the king had taken off his mask and showed her the face of her father. Fear had ruled them both for so long. Aoife bit her mouth to shut off the frustrated scream threatening to erupt. Fear would no longer rule her, it had stopped her for so long from living.

She all but ran from the room, not waiting to see if Malcolm followed her. Without pause she headed out toward the wide expanse of forest. Destiny was no longer going to shape her, no one was going to tell her anymore what was expected of her, she was going to take her life into her own hands.

Even if it meant defying her king.

Chapter 16

Aoife bit down the anger she felt inside. The king had done some off handed things to her, and she had forgiven all the actions. She let it go because she knew he was hurting, they both were. Now he was trying to push everything away that she loved, forcing her into isolation because of his pain, his fear.

As she made it to the gate she slowed her pace, the guards posted there blocked her way. They had never done this before; the king must have been thorough about her confinement.

"Let me pass," she held her head up high, straightening her shoulders. Trying to look every part a queen.

"We are not allowed to let you leave the palace unattended." one guard said, he was just a boy.

She bit her tongue as to keep her frustration from unleashing on the boy.

"Well I will be escorted. They will be joining me shortly. Now let me pass."

They stood firm, she could see they were only fidgeting slightly. Aoife was just about to explode when the men stood even more erect, if that was possible. Nodding their heads at the person behind her.

Aoife's face flamed, praying that it was not the king seeing her try to escape. If it was him, he would lock her in her room keeping her from her last true source of comfort.

A deep, peaceful voice spoke. "Let her through, I will go with her. I am sorry I was late princess, I will be here next time."

Liam.

Her shoulders relaxed. Nodding her head and giving the guards a look of superiority, she walked through the gate waiting for Liam to go with her. He grabbed her hand to stop her. Her face burned in embarrassment.

He turned back to the guards who stood as if a rod replaced their spines.

"Next time the Princess wants to leave allow her through. I will never be too far away, if that pleases the king."

They walked straight to the woods, his hand still holding hers as the fire colored leaves shielded them from view.

Aoife let her hand drop from Liam's grasp when she felt they were far enough away, folding her arms. Liam watched her with calculating eyes, not saying a word. Leading her to her mother's spot. She refused to speak, it didn't seem to bother him though. He sang in that same unfamiliar language. The tension in her head began to ease.

Aoife noticed that the trees were full of deep reds, oranges and gold filling the branches, circling them in a world of colors. The sky which could only be seen through the breaks in the leaves was sea gray, a clap of thunder rang across the sky.

"It will not be long until the leaves fade and fall to the ground," Aoife spoke aloud, though more to herself.

"When they start to fall, our lessons will be over. Their absence will create space for anyone to see what we are up to. And if it is all the same to you, I would like to stay on your father's good side."

Aoife took that in, when the trees start to weep and shed their colors, that is when she will meet her prince. The man who is supposed to save the kingdom from all the threats that are circling Aoife and her father. *Would he be able to do it?* She wondered.

She nodded, "It will be just as well. Who knows what my betrothed would think any way."

Liam seemed not to hear her and moved to grab her sword from its hiding place.

"Are you ready to begin?" Liam interrupted her thoughts. The anger boiled again as she nodded her head yes.

He handed her the blade. She took it in her hand, the feel of it already more comfortable than before. Instead of reviewing like Aoife imagined he would do, Liam started to teach her different protective stances. How to hold your position whether on the offensive attack or defensive.

"Face that tree and strike it as hard as you can. Attack it from all angles, use all the stances I showed you. Force it to bend to you."

"Are we not staying on the drills until I have them mastered?"

He smirked at her, "in battle you learn fast or you die. Now strike the tree."

"How will that help me?" Aoife asked.

"Someone will always be stronger than you. Faster than you. Better than you. You need to be able handle the force at which they will come at you. Now start," his voice seemed distant, annoyed.

She was hesitant at first, it seemed pointless to her. Her arms whined and hissed, and she would not relent, not until Liam told her to stop. Liam barked out different defensive positions, but soon his voice faded into the background lost in the sound of her breathing. Her father's voice ringing in her ears as he closed off all avenues to her freedom. She clenched her teeth as she hacked harder at the tree, shards of bark flying off in all directions.

For years she had put up with the king and his fears. No matter how suffocated she felt, she always found a hole to breathe through, to make it through. The father of her childhood was fearless, kind and most of all he loved her.

When she lost her mother, her father left her too. Devoured by the king. What was left was a hardened version of the man she knew. The tree in her vision became blurry.

Warm hands wrapped around her arms, ceasing her chaotic movements. She turned to face Liam, his blue eyes looking down on her with concern. A breeze tickled her face, making her aware that her cheeks were wet.

She pushed away from him and dropped the sword on the ground. She noticed that her hands were on fire and looked down, red welts covered her palms, scratches from the flying bark lined her arms. She hadn't even been aware of that pain, for the one she carried in her heart was heavier than all of it.

Her breathing was uneven, and she covered her face as if she were hiding herself.

Liam approached her slowly, watching her closely. As a hunter would approach a feral animal. Aoife wiped her face dry, looking at her feet.

"I-" her face was flaming, she could feel the heat in her ears. She was expecting him to scold her or to laugh.

"May I see your hands?" he spoke softly as if not to spook her. She glanced at him, sucking in her breath. Hesitantly, she raised her hands away from her body, they were shaking slightly. Whether from the burst of emotion or for fear of Liam's judgement she couldn't say.

He held her hands gently in his, he stayed silent. She tried to pull them away from him, but he gripped them holding her in place. Aoife's stomach flipped, from emotions that were crashing inside of her.

She laughed shakily, "What a mess I made. I am sorry if I ruined your blade. I can have it fixed."

Liam gently rubbed her palm before answering. "Why do you do that?"

"I don't know what you mean," she retorted flatly.

He allowed silence to dance around them, he just moved away from her, letting her hands drop to her sides. He walked over to the cloth that kept the other weapons in it. Aoife heard cloth ripping. When he came back he had two pieces and wrapped each of her hands. Liam placed his hands on either side of her as if to hold her still.

"It is not good for a person to hold in feelings. Does not help them one bit."

"It's who I am" Aoife said defensively, folding her arms.

"It is who you learned to be. But it does not have to be a part of who you are becoming."

"And who is that? Since you seem to know more about me then I do."

He smiled slightly, "Wouldn't be right for me to spoil the surprise. That is also a part to the story I enjoy, the hero finding out who she is."

He was changing her words? She scoffed, "don't you mean the hero will find out who he is?"

"No, if I meant that I would have said it."

"I don't understand."

He grinned at her "Believe in yourself, you will figure out what I mean."

He let her go and her heart seemed to be pricked by pain at the distance he had created between them. *Why was everyone telling her to believe in herself?* She murmured inside her heart.

"Move over to the next tree, start again," he said as he sat down against the tree Aoife had just maimed.

"You will still teach me?" she whispered, she looked at him in amazement.

He nodded his head and waited until she took her stance next to the tree. Once again Liam had calmed the raging storm she had inside. To her horror, she realized she loved him for it.

She didn't think that the prince of Laoch would find that fact too interesting.

Chapter 17

Rain soaked the earth, like a child's tears on a mother's apron. Aoife watched the rain fall in its steady stream, the damp smell of leaves and wood wafted in her direction. She sat on her chair staring out her window. Muffled sounds reached her ears; servants running, swords clashing, her fire crackling. It was loud, and she welcomed it.

Aoife had not seen Liam for a few days, the rain had been persistent in keeping everyone indoors. Normally Aoife loved the rain, it was perfect weather to curl up by her fire with a good book. Maeve usually would have joined her.

Today she felt agitated with each drop of rain. Would it keep her from her lessons with Liam? She wondered if Liam enjoyed the rain.

Her face burned red, why would she care about if Liam liked the rain? She should be thinking about her betrothed, but she knew nothing of him. Did he ever wonder about her? Perhaps he remained too busy to worry about things like that.

She leaned forward resting her head on her arms on the window sill. Letting the crisp air cool her cheeks. She looked over to her bed. The book Neasa had asked her about ended up being a gift from Liam, it was a picture book of different stances for fighting. Aoife spent all night reading it, not being able to sleep. Her thoughts were filled with Liam all night. Closing her eyes, she slipped into unconsciousness to the sound of the rain.

***

He smelled of the forest. She could not see his face, he held tight to her arm, taking her far from the castle. The moon lit a dim path as they journeyed further into the woods. When did Aoife start to associate him with her woods, her home? They walked briskly, he gripped her arm as if he were afraid she would get lost.

"What is it Liam? What is wrong?" Aoife sounded foreign to herself, her speech was slow. As if she had to say every word with great force.

"They are coming."

"Who is coming? Liam I am scared," Tears flowed down her cheeks. He swung her around to face him.

"They will kill us all. We are dead because of you," his voice was cut off by a snarl as he fell to the ground.

"Liam? LIAM!" Aoife screamed dropping to her knees, shaking him. She threw her body over his, to protect him from what? She frantically looked all around her, the shadows seemed to crawl towards her. Until it grabbed her ankles, the shadows morphed into a man. He was faceless.

His voice was gravely as he spoke, "how sad, but sacrifices must be made." His eyes remained hidden, but his bright grin flashed through the darkness.

"How many more will you let die?" he went on, off to the right the shadows shifted again, showing Maeve her fairy face marred by claws, her eyes glossy as they investigated the eternities. Malcolm was wrapped around Maeve, his skin was gray, death having already passed over him.

Her father at the feet of the stranger in front of her. The stench of death penetrated the air as Aoife heard the sobs and cries of others. The forest was on fire and still the man remained faceless.

Aoife screamed, looking for Liam's sword. The shadow gripped her wrist. Making a hissing sound with his teeth.

"Now my dear, do not pretend to be strong, you will join them soon enough."

Sobbing she whispered, "who are you?"

"Do you not recognize your own husband?" The shadow molded into a new creature. A wolf, his sharp teeth glinting at her the reflection of the burning woods in his eyes. He pounced at her.

***

Her screams woke her up, Liam was peering at her, his hands on her back. She flinched involuntarily. He looked irritated.

"Bad dream?" he asked, his brow raised.

She breathed shakily as she looked around. Her neck ached from being in that position for too long. She rubbed her neck, as she let her racing heart slow down. She didn't answer him for a time. Her mind trying to process the dream.

A dream, that is all it was. Was it an omen that her marriage was wrong? But even the prince of Loach's men were killed. Hundreds were slaughtered. What did it mean? She shook her head, clearing it of the darkness that entered her mind.

"Bad dreams just remind us to be thankful for the good," she smiled tentatively, her mind still whirling about the possibilities of her dream. She almost forgot Liam's hand on her back until he shifted it.

"Was it about that night?" his voice was strained, his anger barely hidden.

She tilted her head and looked into his eyes. The bright blue that captured her attention every time she saw him. He was holding something back from her, his eyes were like locked doors, she could only see the door itself, not what lay behind it.

"No. No Liam, it was just my imagination running wild," she gripped his hand in her urgency to get him to understand. "You have helped me overcome that nightmare. -What I mean to say is you are helping me to- just thank you Liam. I am in your debt, if there was anythi-" She cut off, not knowing why she was rambling. Just needing him to understand that he was helping her.

Realizing how close she was to him made her heart pound she needed to distance herself from him. "I am sorry if I caused worry. I am fine now. It was only a dream."

He nodded, serious again. "I didn't just come in here because you were screaming, it is time for our lessons."

This time Aoife smiled genuinely, "really? I thought because of the rain-"

"Rain is the best time to learn balance in a fight." He smiled back at her, it was a small relaxed smile. It surprised her how real it felt, as though he had never smiled in his life. Her heart pounded, not from fear like it normally did. But the warmth from it filled her body. She was excited, she told herself as she grabbed her cloak and followed him into the woods.

Though she had told Liam it was only a dream, it sat heavy on her heart. She allowed it to drive her in her lesson. She pushed harder than she ever had before.

Chapter 18

"You did well," Aoife could hear the amusement in his voice.

Sweat rolled down her shoulder blades, soaking the back of her dress. Her golden hair was clingy desperately to her face, threatening to loosen its hold on her at any moment. She collapsed on the ground, her muscles hummed with use. She laid there to even her breathing, smiling to herself at the freedom and strength she felt.

Aoife could hear Liam walking on the twigs, it was a quiet footfall. Like a wild animal who stalks quietly to not alert his prey. He sat down next to her, Aoife could feel him next to her, the hairs on the back of her neck stood up. This caused her heart to pound harder, which was the opposite of what she wanted.

She peered at him through half-open eyelids. She found that he was observing the area around them. Her heart sank in her chest, always doing his duty. Of course, he wouldn't be looking at her, how stupid of her. She was engaged to marry his prince.

"You have improved greatly this week," he commented. His eyes never looking at her, but his mouth twitching upward. It looked as if it pained him to do so. Aoife sat up and faced him. Really looking at him, how could he feel like home in her dream? And she didn't know him at all. Over time he had become a friend, and she knew nothing of him.

She ran her hands through her hair to smooth out the knots that formed in her hair, undoing her braid. She smiled more broadly at him.

"Am I good enough yet to join your band of warriors?" She teased.

"Not yet, though I suspect with time you would give Killian a run for his money," he looked at her now, it startled Aoife how much his stare penetrated her heart. It was like he was seeing her soul. She had to look away.

"Now you are teasing me."

"I would not flatter you, I mean what I say." He retorted.

"My father would never approve even if I did become good enough."

"You won't be in your father's care for much longer. It will not be up to him."

"Would the prince allow me to?" She wondered out loud. She glanced at him, hoping he would take the bait.

His eyes glanced skyward, "Do you need his permission?"

"Hmm...that all depends. If my betrothed is like my father now, yes. I would be still locked up in my tower. If he was like my father before…" she drifted off, her thoughts carried her away. Each thought tangling itself up in each other and mocking her.

"Aoife, I have, uh, known the prince a long time, you could say we think… similarly. So, trust me when I say that you will be able to do as you please. You will not be locked up, as you put it," he looked uncomfortable, but his words were firm.

She held his gaze and hoped what he was saying was true. She wanted a marriage like her parents had. No matter how bitter her father was now, the bitterness had sprouted out of a great love for her mother. They were one half of the same whole.

"Besides," Liam continued standing now. "If he does tell you what to do, put him in his place. It will be good for him." He smiled at her and winked. He lowered his hand to help her up. "We have a little light left in the day, should we go again?"

She gripped his hand, churning these details in her mind.

"Unfortunately, I must go back. Neasa will be waiting for me, I have final fittings before the festival."

"That is at this week's end?"

"Aye" She said softly. A new sadness burned itself into heart. "Liam, I think this is the last time we will meet. Soon your prince will be here, and I don't know if I can get away."

"Don't fret, there is one more thing I would like to teach you. We will have to sneak away," He winked at her again. She laughed at his boldness.

As they were walking back Aoife sighed happily to herself, if only Maeve could have joined her. Her smile faltered thinking of her friend. She hoped she was safe beyond the boundaries of the castle walls. She hoped all her people were safe. A chill ran down her spine as she thought of the threat outside Saibhreas land.

Since her argument with her father she had not seen him, and that was the last she had heard about the unrest that happened outside her village.

"Are you cold?" Liam asked.

"No. I.." her voice died away as the wind rose. The trees hushed her as the wind threw her hair in her face. A cloud of foliage twirled around them brown had replaced the vivid colors. Aoife imagined the farmers would be gathering the end of their crops. Maeve would soon be free to practice her trade and soon Aoife would be married.

Aoife couldn't help but think her friend got the better end of the deal.

Aoife giggled trying to desperately clear her face if the hair that lingered there making her blind to the world around her. She felt tugging on her hair. Liam had parted her hair from her face and tucked some of her golden strands behind her ear. The cold she felt was replaced by the fire growing in her belly. He unnerved her.

"What made you shiver Aoife? If not the cold," his voice whispered as dusk started to fold around her. She pulled her hood over her head concealing the emotions behind the protection of her hood.

"I am worried. Maeve is far away from me and the invaders are advancing toward our land. I just...I worry that the people do not have enough defense. And then there is the festival. I feel as if too much is coming at once..." She faded, her thought trailing ahead of her tongue.

"Maeve will be safe, trust that your father has set up precautions. That is why I am here, to protect you and your people. Besides soon they will have their queen to protect them too." He shrugged while smiling in her direction.

"I should trust that Malcolm wouldn't let anything happen to Maeve."

He chuckled in response.

She tried to see her reflection through his eyes. "Do you really mean it? Will I be a good queen?"

"There is still a lot you need to know. But you are a quick learner, it comes naturally to you." Aoife's heart felt as though it would sing right through her chest. She clapped her hands together in glee.

"Your father would be proud of you."

Her heart screeched against her chest. She forced herself to keep her voice light and unattached.

"King Eamonn would not...approve. He thinks that I am better off...in his- in the castle."

"You do not give your father enough credit." He chided.

Aoife stopped in her tracks. "Do not pretend you know everything about the King." She said angrily.

He stood to face her, neither one afraid to speak their mind.

"You should take your own advice. You do not know everything, that is true. I may not agree with your father and how he chooses to exclude you. Trust me, there is more to him than you give him credit for. He cares for you. He just has an odd way of showing it." Liam said.

Disbelief and disappointment were her allies. Liam was her friend why was he taking the side of the King and claiming that he knew more about his heart than her. The king was her father how would she not be able to see him clearly. She knew him best of all she started to think and stopped herself. She really hadn't known him in years.

Not wanting to give Liam the satisfaction that he was right Aoife decided to change the subject.

"Why were you picked to come here?" she asked walking slowly again toward the castle.

"What?" His voice was tight.

"Why did the prince send you? Wouldn't his best warrior be missed? What about his own lands?"

"Laoch is defended. You were higher on priorities for...the prince."

"Hmm..." So, the prince was wanting to defend his new land.

She bit her lip, stuffing down what she was thinking. She knew it was not fair to the prince to always think such nasty things of him. She couldn't help it. In her heart she wanted Liam and she hated it. She didn't think any man, prince or not, could measure up to Liam.

"I can tell that you are holding something back. What is it?" He asked.

Liam saw her so clearly. Unnerved, she couldn't have him know that her thoughts were a battle between loving him and the promise she made to his prince. Liam was a man of duty and wouldn't understand her. How could he? He didn't feel the same way.

"Liam...I never thanked you for helping me with...everything. I will make sure the prince knows what you have done for me. You will be greatly rewarded." She stopped to face him, she gripped his arm to stop him as well. Her heart swelled, and her throat felt as if though it would close to stop all her breathing.

"Rewards are not important to me," Liam clipped and kept walking. Startled by his reaction Aoife ran to keep up with him.

"Whatever you want will be yours Liam. I promise."

His blue eyes flashed as he walked, tension was strapped to his shoulders as tight as vines to a wall.

"Will the prince not feel free to reward you? I am sure I can talk him around."

"Please stop mentioning the prince," his voice sounded strained. With the castle gates in sight he fell silent as he led her inside her prison. Malcolm was there to greet them both, his eyes narrowed at their expressions.

"Lovers spat?" Malcolm teased.

"Hardly," Liam said through clenched teeth. Aoife's face flushed.

Their gazes fixed past her, back into the woods. Their muscles tightened, and Liam stepped closer to Aoife shielding her. She heard him swear underneath his breath. Killian looked overjoyed as he sauntered up to the small group. His eyes glinted coolly as he gazed at all of them. His lips curled cruelly into what resembled a smile. He walked straight to them. His eyes never straying from Liam's face.

"Sir, I found these in the woods, I thought you would want them back before the storm. I wouldn't want them to get ruined," he said innocently. He handed Liam a bundle. "Wouldn't want the wrong kind of people to find these. That is just helping to make the princess an easier target than she is now," his eyes held hers and his smile tightened.

Aoife's stomach dropped to her feet. Bile rose to her throat. She resisted the urge to flinch.

Killian bowed as he placed her sword in Liam's hand.

What big teeth you have.

The better to *devour* you with my dear.

Chapter 19

Aoife's heart leapt within her chest. Her lungs refused to expand as her body responded to what Killian had unearthed. Aoife felt her face fall into an easy smile, but she had to look away for she could feel the panic that exploded in her eyes.

Liam took the sword in hand as he thanked Killian. Aoife's stomach churned.

"Malcolm, let us go to the kitchen I am feeling very hungry," her tone she kept light as her tongue felt like rock in her mouth, weighing down her jaw.

She held her head high as she walked away from all the men of Laoch, leaving them in gazing after her. She prayed that Killian would keep his lips sealed and only think that it was Liam's forgetfulness.

She could not help but feel that the end was near.

***

"Maeve sends her love. She also said to tell you that she was fine and to not worry." Malcolm clapped his hands together waking Aoife from her thoughts.

"Ah there you are. I wondered if a fairy woman had stolen your mind right before me. Liam would not have been pleased." Malcolm bit into a crisp apple. His frame filled the doorframe to the kitchen. He leaned against the wall as if he were trying to be out of the way, but his large frame would not allow it.

A pang of jealousy hit Aoife that Malcolm could be with her friend, but she could not. As she gazed on him though he seemed very content and she wondered how well they were getting on. If only she could talk to Maeve herself.

"Do you agree with her? Is she safe," Aoife mumbled to Malcolm, looking at the food in front of her. She pushed it away and folded her hands securely in her lap. Raising her eyes to his.

"Aye. All is well," his voice sounded as if he too wanted to believe it. Believe that everything was alright.

Aoife feared that the silence was only a calm before the storm rages.

She stood up needing to find Neasa knowing that the woman would be worried about her. As well as, desperate to find her to finish the fittings. They had barely left the kitchen when a young boy came running down the halls calling for Malcolm.

"Sir I am supposed to retrieve you." He said between gasps, he looked at the princess. "There is a problem."

"What is happening?" Aoife asked trying to hide her irritation. More secrets.

"All I was told was to get the Sir, princess." the boy squeaked.

"No matter, I will be in my room," she nodded toward Malcolm then turned to continue with her original plan to find Neasa.

Aoife decided to wander the halls, too irritated to be around the motherly Neasa, she hoped that all was well in the Kingdom. She heard her father's voice muffled voice traveling through the door, he sounded angry. Aoife shrunk back, debating whether to turn around, until she heard Liam's voice. *What could they possibly be discussing?* She inched closer to the door, looking through the crack, trying to hear them better.

"My daughter is not one of your warriors! She is just a girl. We agreed that you would come to protect Aoife not lead her further into danger!" her father hissed.

"She is not glass, my King. She will not break being confronted by a challenge. In my kingdom women are starting to fight alongside the men. Aoife is bringing new ideas and insights and she is becoming aware of other people's needs ahead of her own. New thinking is what your kingdom needs," his voice never rose, but there was a warning in his voice.

King Eamonn's eyes fell into slits.

"What my kingdom needs is strength. Which is what you are here for, not to recruit my daughter into the fight." His voice was ice.

"The fight is coming to you whether you want it to or not. It is at your very doors knocking. You can't see that though; your fear makes you blind. Just as your keeping your daughter in the dark it is blinding your daughter. She must be allowed to see clearly the tasks that are before her, let her rise to the occasion. She may surprise you. But I beg you not to leave her in the dark."

"Do NOT tell me what is best for *my* daughter."

Both men had reached a calm in their tone that sent shivers down Aoife's spine. She looked through the crack in the door and into the room. They both looked tired. Guilt slid into Aoife's stomach like lead. For her idea she got Liam in trouble.

"Do your duty boy. Leave my daughter be."

The door Aoife was leaning on fell forward, causing her to almost lose her balance and placed her between the King and Liam. Her face flushed red. Liam could not meet her eyes. Her father gripped her upright. Killian looked more amused than ever.

So, he was the snake that caused this mess. She wished she could slap that smirk of his face. Clutching her hands at her side, she could hardly breathe.

The old king sighed as he released his daughter.

"Father please let me learn to fight. I am getting good at it. If you just-"

"If I just WHAT? You are NOT fighting! Ever. That is the end of this nonsense." King Eamonn bellowed.

She swallowed hard against the lump in her throat.

Liam stepped forward his mouth opening in Aoife's defense. "Aoife has a mind of her own. Let her decide her own path."

The king whirled on Liam, his finger pointed right in Liam's face. "Know your place boy, you are not yet King here!"

Aoife's stomach dropped. She looked between King Eamonn and Liam as they stared daggers at each other. Killian's mouth dropped into a wicked smile. The room started to spin under Aoife's feet. She clutched at her eyes, trying to process what was said.

"Why would he be king here?" Aoife asked. Silence. She looked at Liam.

"Think hard princess why would Liam become the King of this country? We know you can piece it together." Killian mocked.

She stepped back toward the hall. "Y-you are the prince of Loach." It was not a question.

He moved toward her. "Aoife, I-"

She stepped away and smacked into someone. She turned her shaking body to see who it was and found Malcolm worry etched across his face.

"My Lords, the village is under attack."

They heard screaming echoing through the halls. Aoife rushed to a window and saw a fire growing just beyond her forest. It cast up smoke into the sky making a haze around the sky. No doubt the castle was emptying while people hurried to the village.

Maeve. Aoife pushed past Malcolm into the hall she ignored the shouting of her name. Who called for her she couldn't tell. She kept running, out the door, past the gate and into the woods.

Branches cut into her arms and dress, she still didn't stop. She kept running pushing past the burning of her lungs until she reached the village. She listened to her breathing and ran almost blindly through the trees. A loud choked laugh escaped her throat, Liam had secrets as well. She resisted the urge to scream, it wasted energy and would alert people of her coming. What were they trying to do? Her father and his blasted plans for her! She allowed the anger to push her forward.

When she cleared through all the trees, smoke entered her lungs and her breathing already shallow from running would remain so until she could get some clear air. She bent down and ripped a piece of her dress long enough to tie over her mouth to keep as much smoke from her lungs as possible. The light from the fire hurt her eyes. Ash covered her like a gentle snowfall, from rooftops to the market place all had been made into kindling for one big bonfire of her kingdom.

The village was in chaos. All the confusion made it possible for Aoife to be invisible to the guards that flew around her. Children were screaming, men grunting. Aoife pushed through into the clearing. Women gripping their children close to them, dragging them away from the flames. Some men were trying to stop the flames, while others were gathering the women and children together.

She could hear them all coughing, she moved off to the side where the women and children were being told to stay. Without thinking she ripped more fabric from her dress and placed them on the nearest children's mouths.

She called their attention to her. "You shouldn't inhale this much smoke. Cover your airways with a fabric. Help others to do the same!" She appointed some of the women who weren't as hysterical to oversee making sure that everyone in this group had their mouths covered.

"Maeve!!" She yelled. She desperately looked around in the faces for that of her friend.

Aoife turned to a woman next to her, "What happened?"

The sobbing lady was making herself sick.

Aoife grabbed her shoulders to keep her from falling to the earth. "Please," She inquired gently "what happened?"

"Men- in masks-" she said between gasps of air. Out of the corner of her eye she saw two children by the feet of the lady. They looked up with grave eyes. She bent down to the children she could see the fright in their eyes. She patted their cheeks and smiled at them. She spoke in soothing sounds, like when Liam tried to calm her down. She unfastened the cloak from around her neck and placed it around the young family.

Right then men from Laoch charged in on their horses. Liam was at the front, Aoife shrunk away from him into the shadows, King Eamonn was not too far behind. Liam was shouting, no doubt trying to create some order among his men.

She wondered if they had known about the men in the masks. Leaning to one of the young girls who seemed calm, Aoife told her to tell the king of the attackers.

Aoife then slipped through the crowds, careful to avoid the king's and Liam's. Aoife's eyes searched all the faces of those around her for that of her friend. Occasionally calling out her name.

Maeve's house was in the back of the town, a small cottage that fit a lot of children. Aoife would always tease Maeve that her house would burst at the seams with that many people in one tiny place. What was always so full of life now looked like a corpse in the hazy moonlight. Only shadows filled the walls now.

Aoife in her panic took off running to the home of her friend. She called inside with only echoes of her voice as the return answer. The memory of her dream came back to her. Panic overtook her in that moment, just as she was about to call out again she heard a break of a branch under someone's feet. She slipped in between the shadows and the walls and moved away from the voices. Rough and deep murmurs filled the space around her.

"Who ordered you here?" A rough, familiar voice asked.

Aoife saw that it was Killian in relief she moved to step out to him just as she was about to call his name she saw a mask glint off the fire's light. She retreated further into the house.

"We are getting tired of waiting, we want him dead. We will not wait forever." The second voice retorted, he sounded annoyed more than anything.

"This is what you call waiting?" Killian hissed. "Tell your chief that he will get what he wants if you all follow my plan. You get your jewels I promised and Laoch get more land to expand our kingdom."

Aoife's heart dropped to her feet. Liam? What did he have to do with all this. Was he the one who set this up?

"For your sake, I hope so."

"Are you threatening me?" Killian sounded amused.

"Well I don't see pretty boy backing you up. My chief is starting to think you will get us all killed."

"That pretty boy will come around. He wasn't set on marrying the girl anyway. His father wanted to expand." He shrugged. "Any way I cut it I come out the hero."

"What will you do with the brat?" the man said deflecting the question.

"Well since you failed to throw her from her window. Leave her to me. Dead or alive she does not harm anything. Maybe your chief will want her for a bride."

Aoife lay her head against the wall and closed her eyes. Nausea settled around her. They never found her attempted captor because Killian was working with him. Two times tonight she had been in the wrong place at the wrong time. Neasa always did tell her that listening to conversations that she wasn't apart of would get her into trouble. Aoife made usually made a habit to stay out of the way and out of trouble. She pinched her nose between her fingers. *What was she to do when trouble came to find her?* Neasa never prepared her for that.

If he thought he was going to marry her off, he had another thing coming. Aoife needed to tell Liam and King Eamonn.

Aoife could not hear the voices any more she slowly approached the door. She breathed deeply and counted to three when she flew from the house she smacked right into Killian.

"Eaves dropping princess?" Killian's silhouette was outlined by the moon. His eyes reflecting the light from the burning village before him.

Aoife stepped backward being forced back into the house of her friend. He moved toward her slowly as if he was savoring a great feast. His eyes gleamed in the night's faint light, the hairs stood on her neck.

"I don't know what you mean, I was looking for my friend." She fidgeted with the hem of her sleeves. He stepped forward, she stepped back. Clicking his tongue to censure her.

"Now princess lying gets you nowhere."

She ran into a table.

"Aren't you a hypocrite to say that to me." She was so tired of being afraid, she stood taller.

He laughed "So you were listening. Tis' a shame it has to be this way." He moved to grab his sword from his belt.

Aoife groped the table behind her for anything to use, her fingers touched a smooth surface. She quickly crashed the object down on Killian's head, he stumbled backwards giving her enough room to run from him.

When she came closer she saw the lady she left with her cloak and saw the king had it in his hands. Her body felt frozen, a group of villagers looked on at their king.

"Woman where did you get this? Where is the girl who gave you this cloak?" His voice was tight, but calm. That seemed to add to the fear of the woman.

The woman was trembling and kneeling at the feet of the king. She gasped that she didn't know. "I am sorry my king, I was too frightened! I was not in my right mind." The children coward at their mother's side. The woman bowed to the ground, trying to hide her face.

Raising her chin higher, Aoife stepped into the crowd and called to the king.

"My king I am here." She tilted her head in his direction. She then moved toward the woman to help her stand. "this kind lady was helping me keep my cloak warm. I am sorry to cause you trouble father, but I went in search for Maeve."

"She is not a concern of mine," he turned away from her, barking at one of the soldiers to take her home.

Heat rose to her face at the chastisement from her father in front of their people. She held her tongue so as not to cause more despair. She closed the distance between the king and her. She grabbed her cloak and whispered to him.

"Father might I stay and help, these are our people. If I could be of assistance-"

"Go home. That is where you can help."

"Listen to me father I know who-"

"Look around you daughter. Look at the suffering and the fright in the people. You are making this worse," his voice was strained but he never went louder than for her ears to hear. "Go home." Waving the guard forward, he turned away from her bellowing out orders.

She tasted metal in her mouth she bit down too hard on her lip. The guard came advanced toward her with his horse. He had dismounted and lead her back to the horse, he was about to lift her up in the saddle when he stopped.

"I will take her home," a familiar voice said.

Aoife wanted to cry and run away all at once. The frozen air of the night danced in her hair trying to tug it free from the braid. Aoife could smell the promise of a storm in the air. She couldn't look him in the eye, though Killian had said Liam was not a part of this destruction he had said that Liam would thank him one day. Confliction eclipsed in her heart. Could she trust Liam?

"Aoife, what happened to your dress?" His warm hand grabbed her own and pulled her closer to him. Those same hands pulled down the fabric she had around her mouth. "is this what you did to your dress?"

She had forgotten about ripping her dress, she fought the urge to play with her skirt to try and cover it up. Instead of responding, she shook her arm free from his grasp. Hurt flashed in his eyes. Her anger flared at the audacity of him to feel hurt, but it died just as quickly. She needed someone to listen to her about Killian before he wormed his way back into her home or worse he found Maeve before she could.

"Liam, I need to know Maeve is alright."

Liam responded by letting out let a low whistle, and then sat in silence as if waiting for a response. Aoife felt the wave of impatience, she was going to ask him if he was ever going to respond. He placed a hand on the small of her back to guide her in a direction that took her away from the path of the castle and deeper into the throng of people.

Aoife looked for the king anxiously, but his mind was now averted elsewhere, she was almost forgotten in his thoughts. Malcolm appeared from the shadows. How did they find each other in all this chaos?

"Do you know where Maeve is?" Liam asked, Malcolm's eyes widened at seeing Aoife, but he quickly answered Liam.

"She was assisting people with their burned injuries. She is just over there," he pointed to the mass of people in the darkness.

Aoife smiled, of course Malcolm would know where Maeve was. Of course, Maeve would be helping. She shook her head slightly to clear her thoughts. Killian's sickening smile flashed before her eyes.

"Malcolm stay with her. Do not leave her side. Killian was behind this and I am afraid that he will hurt her because of me."

Liam and Malcolm shared a glance as if she was confirming something they already knew.

"Did you know about Killian?" her voice rose with each word.

Liam cleared his throat. "We suspected..."

She flinched away from away him. "He was the one who told that man where to find me. They tried to have me killed by failing to throw me from the window! Find him and you'll find the men who tried to burn this kingdom to the ground."

Her head started to pound, she rubbed at her temples.

"Find them," she pointed at both men.

Liam spoke quietly in that same foreign language that he had sung her to sleep. That seemed like years ago now. Malcolm's eyes hardened as whistled low, the same low note Liam had used before they found him. She noticed that men who wore the insignia of Laoch turned toward him and soon Malcolm was surrounded by their men.

"Wait here," Liam grabbed the nearest horse and brought it to Aoife. He lifted her up and sat behind her wrapping his arms tight around her waist. Aoife thought that he was holding on too tight, she tried to loosen his hold by moving around, but he only clutched to her tighter. Liam kicked the horse into a trot as he took off back to the forest. Her heart pounded with each hoof beat against the ground.

So, this was the man she is to marry, she could feel the fire in her blood rush up her neck into her face. The wind seemed to carry them faster home. The castle rose on the horizon to meet them. The tension between them was making her stomach churn painfully. The horse stopped and as Aoife went to slide off the horse Liam's arms fastened around her tighter.

"Aoife take this." He pressed a dagger's hilt into her hands hiding it within the folds of her skirt. "You are a skilled fighter, whatever happens protect yourself."

Aoife looked at him in disbelief. He was always on her side, whatever his kinsman did it was not who Liam was. This time she needed to be on his side. He jumped down from the horse and he wrapped his hands around her waist to help her down from the horse. Even after she was firmly on the ground he continued to hold onto her waist.

"Aoife I really wanted to tell you." He looked desperate.

"I guess I was not the only one with secrets," she whispered to him as she gazed in his blue eyes. She saw him grimace and his shoulders tighten.

"We all have secrets princess its learning to live with them that matters," she could feel the weight of his stare. She felt that what she said next would be weighed deeply by Liam. She gripped her dagger tighter.

"Secrets are used to shelter others from burdens that we feel are our own to bear. Yet they often cast a divide and a heavy burden on the one who is left in ignorance." She said, knowing that she was a hypocrite.

He stepped closer his forehead resting against hers. Her breath caught in her throat her face flushed with heat. She felt herself relaxing in his arms. The guilt from the duty to her betrothed drained away from her. He was one in the same, her whole heart was his.

"It was not my choice," Liam's said hoarsely.

She stepped away from him. How could she forget that they were both pawns in a game? Without another word she walked away from him, she didn't even turn around when he called after her. How could she think he liked her? He was just comforting her, it was his duty after all. She had a maid stay in her room with her that night, to watch over her.

That night she fell into a fitful sleep, hand still clutching the dagger.

Chapter 20

Aoife awoke to her floorboards creaking she was still clutching the handle of the dagger from the night before. Aoife sat upright in her bed and right before she pulled out the dagger. She saw that it was her nurse and the maid from the night before.

Neasa jumped back and yelped in surprise. The old woman clutched at her heart, "goodness child you startled me. I didn't know you were awake." She laid fabrics of every color on Aoife's bed, like before. This time they all were made up into different bodices. Neasa placed her hands on her hips and looked Aoife up and down.

"Are you alright princess? You look as if you've seen the moon goddess herself."

Aoife looked toward her mirror that hung on her wall, her face was drained of color. She laughed shakily pinching her cheeks with one hand trying to draw life into her face.

"Well get out of bed! We must try on these dresses to find the best one for tonight, "The old woman gushed, "we will make the prince wish he had come here a lot sooner."

Everyone was kept in the dark with her about who Liam was. She didn't know if that comforted her or if it made her feel worse.

"I am not sure more time would have made the difference" Aoife muttered to herself.

Realizing she had to hide the dagger she looked around the room for the best place to conceal her weapon.

"Neasa I am famished; would you mind getting me something to eat."

Neasa sent the girl to fetch Aoife something from the kitchen. Neasa looked at Aoife to move from the bed. *Now to get rid of Neasa for a moment.*

"Neasa I also think that I should bathe, will you go fetch some hot water? Please."

Her eyes narrowed in suspicion, muttering something under her breath she left the room. Aoife closed the door behind her and moved to look around her room. She saw her scarlet hood lying on the floor. *The pocket!* She moved to it and replaced the usual book that hid in the pocket with her dagger. Aoife could hardly see its shape within the folds of her cloak. She hung it up in her wardrobe towards the back, to be out of sight from the watchful eye of the nurse.

She could hear voices in the halls coming closer to her door. She ran to her bed and lifted a dress in her hands as a handful of maids entered her room holding a washing tub. Neasa coming in behind with a pot of hot water.

"I got there just in time. They were about to start a pot of soup. I told them to try again because the princess needed her hot water," She smiled triumphantly.

Aoife went to her side and kissed her cheek.

"You've always taken care of me."

Neasa's eyes misted over, she sniffled. "No more of this, I can't have my eyes be red for tonight. Get in while the water is warm."

Aoife got in and allowed herself to relax she listened to the maids as they moved around her room speaking in hushed excited tones.

"You need not contain yourself on my account, please speak freely with each other. I am content to listen," Aoife said closing her eyes as she went deeper under the water getting her hair wet. Lavender was placed in the water, she welcomed its calming influence.

The maids chirped about the repairs on the village, fathers re-patching their roofs, while brothers continued to prepare for the festival around the village's ashes. The women and children were left to clear the debris left behind. All of it was put together by Liam and King Eamonn, Aoife had to admit that they were good in a crisis.

Only when they started talking of the prince and the warriors from Laoch did Aoife shy away from the conversation. One of the girls was brave enough to ask if she was given clues to who she would marry. What the prince looked like. Her face flushed red in humiliation, he deceived her and yet she was the one who felt embarrassed. She shrugged her shoulders. *What he must think of her and her boldness?*

As one girl was putting oils that smelled of flowers in Aoife's hair, Aoife smiled at her and said, "the men of Saibhreas are just as fine of men as those Laoch warriors, but it would be good for them to have some competition."

She laughed as the rest of the maids giggled. She liked that these girls who chatted easily around her, she let their voices distract her thoughts as she was pulled out of her bath. She moved to her dresser, putting on a simple gown.

"Neasa?" She called.

"Yes dear?"

"Send the best girl to deliver my purple dress to Maeve, I want her to wear the best for tonight," Neasa smiled and ordered the girl closest to the wardrobe. Aoife was hoping to give it to Maeve herself, but her father had locked her up and therefore had to make due with her resources. She approached the girl with the dress and linked arms with her as she walked towards the door.

"Saoirse, will you tell Maeve something for me as well?"

The girl nodded eagerly. "Please tell her to find me tonight."

She was startled to see Liam and Malcolm whispering in the hallway. Aoife's face flamed bright red. She wanted to retreat back into her room but stood her ground.

"Hello," she bowed her head at them both and turned her attention to Malcolm, hoping that no one could read the tension in her body. But knowing that Liam did.

"Did you catch my snake?" Aoife asked smiling. The girl beside her was grinning like a fool. No doubt hoping to draw either of their attention. She resisted the urge to tell her they were both taken.

Malcolm looked between her and Liam his eyes had not left her face since she entered the hall.

"Malcolm will you take Saoirse to Maeve for me, I have a delivery and I want to make sure that they all end up safe where they need to go. And after last night..."

"I would be honored," Malcolm looked at Liam they seemed to speak to each other without words. It made Aoife miss Maeve all the more. Malcolm nodded his head as if he had been commanded.

He walked away with Saoirse telling jokes, but Aoife could see the tightness in his shoulders.

Not wanting to be with Liam alone, Aoife pivoted and moved back towards her door. Liam caught her arm and stopped her. She could feel the frustration radiating off him in waves.

"Aoife-" Liam started. She did not want to talk now. Her head was spinning, and she knew that the maids inside her room were listening.

"Did you find anything out on the men from last night?" Aoife interrupted.

"No one saw faces, they all had masks that covered them." He answered.

"Have you found the snake?"

Liam shook his head, "He is hiding. We will find him."

"I just hope it is before more of my people get hurt."

"I promise you, I will protect our people," He whispered stepping closer.

She shivered.

Neasa opened the door, startled to find Liam with his hand around Aoife's arm. The warm old lady turned cold and said, "Kindly remove your hands from the princess."

Liam held his arms in front of him like he was surrendering, Aoife laughed and patted Liam on the arm.

"Dear Neasa, I had tripped. Liam was just helping me, so I did not fall. I will be right in."

The lady looked like she doubted Aoife's words and harrumphed as she walked back into the room.

"I will look into it. Until then stay safe and keep that dagger on you." He walked away, and Aoife went back into her room.

***

Aoife had not left her room for two days. Meals were brought to her and Neasa stayed close, watching her like a hawk. No doubt her father had something to do with the prison sentence. Aoife passed the time with reading and sleeping. Boredom hung around her as a stench might.

The day of the festival came and after hours of being poked and prodded by needles, Aoife was ready for the festival. Her light golden hair was loose flowing down her back in waves. She wore a white dress that flowed down her body with a scarlet ribbon tied at her waist. Her blue eyes stood out contrasted against the paleness of the dress. When Aoife looked at herself she was startled to see her mother staring back at her, it took her a minute to recognize herself.

Neasa walked to the wardrobe collecting the red cloak that hung lifeless. Aoife prayed that the woman would not feel the weight of the dagger in her pocket. Lucky for Aoife the woman was too occupied with gushing over her, that she did not pay attention.

Neasa wiped away her tears and nodded approvingly, commanding all the other ladies to leave and get ready themselves. Their cheery voices were left behind as the girls practically ran down the halls. Neasa started to shut the door, coming over to Aoife.

Aoife could hear the drums beating from the village, a knock sounded at her door. it was time to leave.

Neasa hugged her tightly and patted her face with her rough palm.

"You look beautiful little one. Your father will be proud of you."

"I am not sure anything I do will make him proud," she muttered under her breath.

"Hold your tongue! You are not seeing with a clear eye. King Eamonn is as proud as you as I am," she chastised.

"I would not know it. He has not been the same since the day my mother was killed. He-"

Neasa laid her hand on Aoife's mouth to stop her rant.

"Aye lass and I am sorry for it. Losing your mother is a burden no girl should know. But think, is it not just as hard for any man to lose his wife, especially when she was his whole heart. He is grieving in his own way, but that does not mean he loves you less. Try and understand him."

"That is a difficult task," she murmured warmly to woman in front of her. "May I have a minute to myself?"

"Only a few moments my dear, the King would like to escort you to the celebration and we know how he can get in being late." She shook her head as if a memory fluttered across her vision.

Aoife stood still for a moment, as if to capture the time before everything changed. She held her hands to her eyes pressing against the light. She knew her father had suffered, but she never thought to think that his cold exterior was his own from of protection. She needed someone to reach out to her and extend guidance and love. Though he could not give it to her himself, he had given her people who could: Maeve, Rowan, Liam.

She could see now that all of that had been for her. She moved her hands from her eyes. The light of the morning filtered through the window making her blink against the brightness.

Who had been there for her father? He took care of the kingdom and Aoife, whether she knew it or not, but he had no one. She felt ashamed of her selfishness.

The halls were coated in autumn's chill, Aoife could hear the swishing of her skirt as she walked out of the castle to the front gates. King Eamonn must have let all the servants leave already. The hairs on the back of her neck stood up on their ends. Her father stood by two horses, his stern face watched her as she approached. She saw his chest halt and then resume breathing as if it had caught in his throat.

He held out a hand to her and she grabbed her father's hand. "You look so much like your mother. I wish she-"

"I miss her too father." She tightened her grip on her father's arm. They stood sharing their common grief. It was in that moment that Aoife realized that he had been hiding his pain from her, just as she hid hers from him. Instead of relying on the mutual sadness and loss they experienced they walled themselves off, shutting the other one out in the process.

Aoife felt her heart would break from the regret that washed around her. She wanted to move forward with peace and stop looking backwards in bitterness.

"I am sorry for your pain father," she said as she kissed his cheek.

Her father cleared his throat and dropped her hand. The moment snapped, and her father transformed back into the king.

"Stay close to the guards, I don't want to be worrying about you this evening."

"My king look at me."

King Eamonn looked at the woman in front of him, his forehead crinkled in agitation.

"Am I such a burden to you that you can't stand to be in my presence for longer than a moment? I am still here father. But you have not been, the day my mother was taken from me, my father died as well."

"Aoife…"

"I needed you father and now you are sending me away again. I will marry Liam and save Saibhreas. I want to help you father, that is all I ever wanted."

I forgive you for not loving me the way I needed you to. Can you forgive me for being blind to your intentions?

"Daughter, do you love him?" His voice was tight.

Her face flamed. "Yes," she whispered.

Aoife quickly got on her horse and held the reigns, she didn't want to speak on the subject anymore, she didn't know if she should thank her father, because all she really wanted to do was scream at him for hiding this from her. Making her feel like her heart was being toyed with. Aoife could not read her father; his face was still. Without a word he mounted his horse and they rode toward the village, Aoife just felt worse inside telling her father all the pain she has held in for years, again making it about herself.

They reached the edge of the woods; the pale light of the sky warmed her skin. A crunching sound beneath her feet, the trees shed their leaves, embracing the winter that threatened to come. They moved swiftly through the forest, neither one speaking, the village was in front of them. Aoife could hear the humming of voices, she wondered if Killian was among the crowd.

The drums beat louder, people cheering as they rode into the center of the village, welcoming the king and his daughter to the celebration.

Chapter 21

Merchants lined the streets, all that remained of the fire that night was the soot. Warriors from Laoch and her own people intermingled together. Men and women wrapped around each other. Children weaving around people, the sight was as joy itself. The human spirit was the strongest substance on earth Aoife thought. In the center of the village, girls danced about it as if they were possessed by the music. It seemed to twirl with the wind inviting everyone to join in and move to the beat. The music was the master.

Aoife dismounted, and she began to look for Maeve. Malcolm never returned and so she assumed that he stayed with her. With every beat of the drum Aoife's heart thudded more deeply within her chest. Her father went and sat on two chairs that they had for them.

She heard her name being called and turned around to see Maeve running towards her and Malcolm trying to keep up. The sight brought a giggle from her lips as her friend embraced her.

"You look beautiful!" They both cried out and laughed.

The purple dress accented the dark features on Maeve, she looked the whole part of a fairy queen, her long dark tresses falling straight down her back. She looked like nature in human form.

"I tried to find you the other night. Are you alright?" she looked around at her friend trying to see any distress or physical damage. She looked perfect.

"Aye, Malcolm told me. I wish I knew you had been here, I would have tried to see you."

"I should have made sure to see you. I just didn't want to be a bother. How is it being an apprentice?"

Maeve linked arms with her friend as they walked up and down the streets, telling Aoife the details of her studies on healing. The noise was so loud, that if Maeve had been standing any further away from her Aoife would not have been able to hear her. Malcolm trailed lazily behind them.

Maeve looked now and again behind her, smiling at Malcolm. Aoife nudged her friend playfully.

"Are you getting soft? Or did I just see you blush when Malcolm winked at you?"

Maeve laughed, "he is not so bad as I thought."

"What changed?" Curiosity burning inside.

"Well because of you," she playfully nudged Aoife back, "he has been around me a lot. At first, I ignored him, but he kept pestering me with questions about my herbs. It was fun to teach somebody. After that spending time with him wasn't hard, it was actually enjoyable." Maeve smiled.

Aoife was happy for Maeve, she liked Malcolm, she could trust him to watch over Maeve. He seemed to understand that Maeve could not be caged, so he chose to run with her instead. They were equals.

Would she be Liam's equal? Will he be hers?

"I need to tell you something." Aoife said she leaned close to her ear.

"Secrets don't make friends" Malcolm scoffed, pretending to be offended.

"Hmmm perhaps that is true, but they keep dear friends closer." Maeve smiled sweetly at him and led Aoife a space away from Malcolm.

Just as Aoife leaned forward to tell Maeve, she saw Malcolm's easy smile slip into a frown. He looked around as if he had heard something and walked away. It got Maeve's attention too, Aoife saw Maeve take a stuttering step towards him. She stopped remembering her friend and gripped Aoife by the arm. Aoife wasn't the only one who had fallen for a warrior of Laoch.

King Eamonn stood and raised his arms. The dancing and the merriment slowly died and when all is silent he yelled.

"My dear guests, I would like to introduce you to your future king." He stood aside as Liam takes a place by his side, Malcolm close behind him. Aoife blinked her eyes as if to look at Malcolm again.

Aoife looked toward Maeve to tell her that this was the secret she was going to tell. But Maeve nodded her head toward something as if communicating with someone. She clasps hands with Aoife and looked at her and smiles. "Congratulations my friend."

"Maeve? Did you know?"

The fairy queen smiled at her sweetly and released her hand. "Are you pleased it is Liam?"

"I don't know. They lied, that cannot be a good sign."

"I think that was more of your father's wishes than Liam's. You know how your father can be."

"I don't think I am ready for this, I don't know him." Aoife said.

"Even if you had a hundred years you might not know all that resides in that man. Look at his actions, those are just physical displays of his mind and heart."

"Who told you?"

"Malcolm told me before the fire. I had a hunch..." Her voice trailed off.

Maeve had known before her. Aoife pinched her forehead in between her hands, a small ache had started there.

Maeve elbowed Aoife in the side.

"Ouch!"

It was then that Aoife realized the crowd whispered in hushed tones. She looked up and her face flamed, Liam was beside her, his arm extended. Without thinking she took his hand. The wolf insignia on his chest seemed to wink at her in the firelight. The beat of the drums filled the air as Liam and her danced.

He pulled her closer to him, as if to keep what was spoken between just the two of them. "I wanted to tell you so many times."

She could feel his hands twitch as if keeping them from bawling into a fist. Aoife's body hummed at his closeness. Liam was her king. But he lied, they all had lied to her.

"Aoife, I know you must be disappointed-"

"At first I was..." She said honestly. She could feel the eyes of the king on her along with the hundreds of other eyes watching the future rulers dance together.

His eyes bore into her own, she felt exposed when she was with him, and it scared her how safe she felt with him. It scared her that she was not mad.

Other people joined in the dance.

"How long were you both going to hide it from me?"

"Your father wanted to wait until tonight, I agreed with him. At the time I thought it to be the right course for you and me both."

"How?"

"Our kingdoms need this alliance. Laoch would defend and your kingdom has wealth beyond any other kingdom. To combine would be beneficial to both sides. Your father wanted to make sure that you could love me before he agreed to you marrying me. I wanted the same decency. And if you didn't like me then we would move on with our lives and your father would find another compromise between him and my father." He shrugged his broad shoulders.

Her father did that for her? Guilt spread across her countenance like the dawn of a new day. She started to pull away from Liam, shame flooding her entire body. Liam held tight to her, encircling her in his arms, she could feel his breath on her face. She could only bring her eyes to his neck, she didn't want to look into his eyes. Aoife was afraid he might see her truth, that she was in love with him, she was more afraid; however, of him not loving her back.

Did he only think of her as another responsibility of his?

Her breath came out in quick and shallow puffs of air, as she looked at Liam her heart expanded in her chest.

"You are assuming that you know my answer." His brow was raised, challenging her to disagree.

Her face colored she started to squirm under the pressure of his stare. She really should have known that she could not hide from him. He was too observant, or perhaps she was too transparent.

"Aoife I-"

He was cut off by screaming. They looked for the source of the chaos. The crowd around them grew restless, knocking into each other. Liam unconsciously pressed Aoife into his side, as if to shield her. He looked around and let out a low whistle.

Men with masks were dotted throughout the crowd.

"Those are the men from the other night," Aoife whispered breathlessly.

Liam's blue eyes became stormy.

"HE HAS THE KING!" Someone yelled from the crowd.

Killian stood on a platform with the King next to him and held a sword at King Eamonn's throat.

Aoife clutched onto Liam. She heard him curse under his breath.

"SILENCE! Weak fools." He sneered, causing all the screaming to stop.

The men with masks seemed to go to the edge of the crowds. Drawing their swords, they drove everyone to the center of the circle.

Herding the sheep.

King Eamonn's eyes looked calm, pride etched in every inch of his face. Aoife knew her father would not beg for his life.

Neither would her people. Aoife straightened her shoulders.

Liam whistled again in the silence. This time Aoife heard a soft reply.

Killian seemed too busy to notice the call of his people.

Liam leaned down to her ear, "I have men on the outside who can attack from behind."

Aoife's eyes were glued to Killian there was madness in them she had never seen before.

"Do you have the dagger?" Liam asked.

She patted her pocket of her cloak.

The terrified buzzing of her people set Aoife on edge. She needed them to rally. She could hear children crying as they clung to the skirts of their mothers.

"SILENCE!" He bellowed. "Where is the girl. Bring her!"

The crowd shuffled closer to her. Her heart swelled with relief.

Killian clicked his tongue in annoyance. "Don't be fools."

Silence was his reply. His countenance darkened. At his signal the men with masks forced them closer into a circle.

"Give me the girl!"

Killian's blade moved almost imperceptibly Aoife watched as her father's body crumbled to the ground. Aoife choked back a sob as all the people cried out. Killian had killed her father.

Liam gripped her arm, she could feel the anger radiating out of him, that anger wrapped itself around her and awoke her body that was frozen with fear.

"Princess, we don't want anyone else getting hurt do we?"

Dull furry spread through Aoife, she wrapped it around herself like a cocoon.

"Whatever happens, get our kingdom back." She said loud enough to be heard by the people around her.

As she walked to the platform the sea of faces parted, giving her what room they could in their tight space. She lifted her chin, hoping no one would notice her legs shaking.

Aoife heard Maeve shouting her name. She drowned out noise pulling strength from the silence.

She climbed the steps and faced Killian, straightening her shoulders. She couldn't look at her father's lifeless form, she clung to the furry that started to spark in her belly.

He opened his mouth to speak and she held up her arm cutting him off.

"Killian do not force my hand. If you surrender to us now, I promise your death will be swift."

His hand struck out smacking her across the face. She saw stars as she fell to the ground. She heard a collective gasp from the audience.

"You? You are nobody."

She shook her head clearing it of the fog and stood up. Her face throbbing, wiping the blood from her lip, she spit at his feet.

The people cheered. She looked for Liam in the crowd she couldn't find him. A faint tune reached her ears, one that she had heard Liam singing before. She took courage, from the shadows the warriors of Laoch emerged, making terrible chanting noises. The commotion caused the intruders to lose the focus, forcing them to turn around and face the surprise force coming down on them. Her people that were rounded up scattered.

At the front of it all leading the men, instinct was driving Liam. At his core he was a warrior, a defender. His blue eyes sparked with a controlled furry. His muscles were coiled, his frame was rigid with anticipation. A predator and prey, a small sarcastic smile formed on Aoife's lips.

The sound of ringing filled the air. The warriors moved as graceful as swans and as deadly as wolves.

His eyes were searching for her, relief washed through her. She was about to call out to him when she was thrown from the platform hitting the ground left her breathless.

Killian loomed over her.

She growled under her breath and clenched her teeth as the pain shot through her body as she attempted to stand. She would no doubt have a lot of bruises when this whole thing was over.

The clear sky was being swallowed by dark storm clouds, it absorbed all the light as they rumbled.

Killian grabbed Aoife by the hair helping her to her feet. She winced as her whole body protested at the movement.

Killian reminded Aoife of a fox. Always taunting its opponents, staying just out of reach. Deceitful and fast creatures. Coward. Foxes were only good for stealing, causing mischief and running back to its hole in the ground.

Aoife reached her hand down to her pocket, she whimpered and pleaded with Killian to have mercy on her. She needed to distract him from what she was doing.

She drove her dagger fast into his side ripping it out again. He released her stumbling backwards.

"You will pay for that." He said through clenched teeth.

Aoife smirked and looked him in the eyes, "you will have to catch me first."

Lightning danced across the sky followed by the bellowing of thunder.

Aoife sprinted towards the woods. She would cut off the head of the snake by herself. A flood of tears fell to the earth. The solid earth quickly turned to mud.

She heard heavy footsteps coming for her. She ran without looking back, driving her deeper into the trees.

She turned off the path leading Killian through the uneven terrain, her hands scraped against the branches. Allowing the shadows and trees enveloping her.

Her mind whirled as she clutched the dagger so as not to lose it.

A force behind her sent her flying into the nearest tree before she fell to the ground. The blade falling out of her grasp. Her side exploded in pain, she gasped for air as she rolled onto her back just in time for Killian to cut her across her thigh.

She hissed, frustration ripped through her as she tried to steady her breathing.

Killian's cruel smile glinted against the darkness.

"Not so fast little one." His eyes danced with cold vehemence, his voice clipped and annoyed. He bent down getting closer to her face, his eyes mocking her.

"You are not fit to rule." He brushed his fingers in her hair, "and you are in my way," he sighed.

Aoife laughed coldly. Her mind raced she needed to get away. She grabbed a handful of mud shoving it into his face.

She frantically felt around for her dagger. The hilt of her dagger glinted, and she lunged for it.

He picked her up by her hood and hauled her to her feet he shoved her against the trunk of a tree her cloak padded the impact.

Now was her chance. With one last effort she plunged the dagger into his arm.

Killian growled in pain.

Aoife took off running back through the trees, she felt disoriented as her body rang with adrenaline, ignoring the searing pain in her leg, she led him deeper into the forest. She prayed that Liam would find her. The rain came rushing down blinding her.

A sharp sting burst in her thigh. She looked to see what knocked her down this time. Warm sticky blood covered her hands as she reached for the handle of her dagger. Her head spun as she ripped it from her leg, hiding it in the folds of her cloak.

She tried to crawl away, and he ripped her backwards by the hood. Laying his sword in it, pinning her to the ground. Her mind raced trying to pull a whirlwind of thoughts into something coherent. She could feel the energy ebbing away.

Killian chuckled as if this was all a great joke. Aoife's white dress was soaked with rain and blood, it was almost indistinguishable from her scarlet cloak.

All she could do was look up into the rain at the face of her father's killer. He bent down he was hovering over her.

She flicked the dagger cutting his cheek. He hissed and backhanded her as the star bursts clouded her vision he took away her last source of life.

"ENOUGH! I am through with these games" He roared. He pressed the knife to her throat pressing until beads of red dripped on the knife.

She stared toward the sky, not wanting to investigate the face of a coward any longer.

"Liam…" she whispered in her heart.

The pressure from her was lifted. She opened her eyes and saw Killian in a heap on the ground, a sword sticking out of his back. She hadn't even heard him approach. Liam pulled his sword from the body, wiping the blood on his sleeve.

"Aoife? Where are you hurt?" His voice was tight as he knelt beside her.

He pulled Killian's sword from her hood, releasing her from her prison. Rain fell down her face, masking the tears that were falling from her eyes. Words failed her, all she could do was watch his as he tore her dress to bind the wound on her thigh.

"Aoife," he says gently. His warm rough hands wiped at her cheeks. She really could never his anything from him.

He picked her up and held her to him as she wept. Her father had died, and she prayed to the moon goddess that her mother had found him. They were together again, now she was alone.

The storm stopped, but her own was just beginning.

She let sorrow consume her.

Chapter 22

Warm light stretched across Aoife's face. She could hear the rushing of the leaves in the trees. Her leg protested the most, throbbing that demanded attention. She opened her eyes to the familiar surroundings of her room.

The events of that night flashed across her memory. She shut her eyes trying to block out the pain in her heart, which worse than any other pain her body felt.

When she opened her eyes again she was staring right into the eyes of Maeve. Maeve's beautiful face was scrunched with concern and pity.

Aoife wept.

Head in her hands she wept for her mother, and her father. Maeve held her in her arms. Aoife clung to her like beggar clung to bread.

Aoife was grateful that Maeve did not try and speak comforting words, she just needed her. Words would be meaningless to her.

Maeve pulled herself away long enough from Aoife to go to the door. She whispered something to someone in the hallway before she returned. Maeve came back and crawled under the blankets with Aoife and held her while she cried.

Deep tenor voices filled the space, Aoife kept her eyes closed wanting to shut out reality for a little longer. Maeve was beside her stroking her hair, calming her.

"She is awake." Maeve said.

Aoife opened her eyes. "Please tell me this was all a dream." She whispered, mostly to herself.

No one answered her. "How are the people? The kingdom?"

Liam stepped forward, kneeling to be eye-level with Aoife. "No one was killed, and any injuries were taken care of by Rowan and Maeve."

"She was always quite the healer." Aoife smiled and felt a tear escape. She brushed it away quickly. She closed her eyes, trying to shut off her emotions. Maeve squeezed Aoife turning to Malcolm.

"Come with me, I need to get more herbs for Aoife's wound and to check on the others who are wounded."

Nodding he said, "I am glad you are safe Aoife."

Maeve linked arms with him as they walked from the room Aoife saw Maeve lean her head on Malcolm, sharing their burden. She smiled then, she never knew who would steal Maeve's heart, but she was glad it was Malcolm.

Liam stood watching Aoife, concern covering his face.

Aoife cleared her throat and her smile faltering, "I uh- I want to thank you for saving me Liam. For saving Saibhreas."

Liam cracked a smile, though it didn't reach his eyes.

"Struggling is a part of greatness Liam. I think they will tell stories of this event for years to come. You know how much I do enjoy a good story." Aoife knew she was rambling now, she didn't know what to say anymore.

"Aye love, you are right about that. Never thought I would marry a hero."

He gripped her hands tighter in his, she flushed. Her heart pounded in her ears. Her eyes pricked with tears returning.

"I don't want to cry anymore. What happened the rest of that night?"

"My men and the villagers fought off the men in masks. Killian promised them a large sum for helping him take down the two most powerful kingdoms. "

"Do we have an enemy?"

"No, they were only the men low enough from other tribes to act out."

"What will we do about the tension among the kingdoms. Surely there's a way to be at peace with our neighbors?"

Liam's eye glinted with hope, and light. His dark hair fell into his face, his usually smooth chin and jaw was covered in stubble. Without thinking Aoife reached up and touched it. Liam smiled.

"I take it you will still marry me then with all this talk of us."

Aoife let her hand drop. She didn't even know that she had been saying we. Her face flamed, and her mouth fell open a little bit.

Liam laughed and kissed her on the cheek. He leaned away from her, so he could look into her eyes.

"Will you still have me?" He asked, his face was finally open to her, allowing her to see him clearly.

"Do you love me?" She whispered, her voice shook. She looked down, suddenly afraid of the answer.

He placed his hands on the side of her face and rested his forehead on hers.

"Aye," his voice was gentle "from that first night I was yours."

With that confession her heart opened, amid all the heartache there was joy.

"Malcolm. He is the one I want to send to smooth over the tribes. But I am afraid he won't do it unless a certain lady joins him."

"Suppose Maeve won't have him?" her mouth curled into a smile.

Liam kissed her on her other cheek. The blush returning to her face.

"I think I can talk her around," Liam kissed her forehead. "Are you alright love?"

"I will be, in time."

"Aye, love. All pain lessens with time."

He kissed her then and wrapping her arms around his neck she kissed him back. Aoife's heart sang in her chest.

The past was to be remembered, the present to thrive in, and the future to be hopeful about.

***

Aoife and Liam married. Aoife could not remain Saibhreas, after the death of her father Aoife could no longer remain where the ghosts of her childhood roamed the halls, too much sadness clung with her there.

Women moved about the castle packing and cleaning the remains of her old life, sorting what must stay and what must go.

Aoife could not stand to watch as they opened up the contents of her house. At the suggestion of Maeve, Aoife went to go for one last walk through her forest. Leaving Neasa and Liam in charge.

"It's okay to be sad Aoife. It does not make you weak to be grieving for the loss of your father,"

The girls walked slowly, arm in arm. Letting the wet of the snow numb their bodies. Aoife let a big puff of air the cloud disappearing just as fast into the crisp air as it formed.

"I am tired of being sad though. Did you know it is more exhausting to hold this weight than to just be happy?"

Maeve clung to her tighter, offering her strength to Aoife.

"Maeve, I do need to ask you something. Will you and Malcolm be married?"

Happiness lit up her face. "Aye, in maybe a month's time. We can't seem to decide where we would live," her brow furrowed together, "I am needed here, who else will take care of the sick? But does that outweigh Malcolm and his life in Loach? It is a hard decision to make, weighing my dreams against the dreams of the man I love."

Aoife could feel the inner conflict in her friend. She had to force down her smile.

"What does Malcolm say?" Aoife asked.

Maeve made an exasperated noise. "He says he really doesn't care. Says it's the warrior inside him, that he is fine so long as he is above the dirt! He can't really mean that can he?"

"One thing that I have learned from Liam and Malcolm is that they don't say anything they don't mean. We have found some good men."

Maeve nodded, distracted by her plague-like thoughts. Aoife was having trouble hiding her smile now. Giggles flew from her mouth.

Maeve looked surprised.

"What is so funny? Did I miss a joke?" She eyed Aoife suspiciously.

"No, it's just..." another giggle, "I may have a solution to your problem. How would you like to stay here with Malcolm and watch over Saibhreas? You would stay here and continue to help people."

Maeve's dark eyes widened in surprise, "are you mad? Me? I could never-"

Aoife pulled Maeve to a stop, looking her in the eyes. "Maeve there is no one I trust more to lead with compassion and fairness. You were the one to open my eyes to all that was happening in my kingdom. It is because of your guidance that I have been able to become who I am."

"I didn't do anything." Maeve looked incredulously.

"You were my friend and that was more than enough." Aoife said emotion tugging at her throat.

Maeve held her arm tighter, they walked on, talking as the snow gently fell around them.

Epilogue

The pressure of joy and stress equally weighed on her bones. Combining the two kingdoms was more difficult than Aoife originally thought it would be. There was always more work into ruling a kingdom than Aoife ever imagined.

They worked tirelessly to build a better kingdom than before, they would be stronger this way. This had caused some difficulties for other tribes surrounding Liam and Aoife.

Aoife felt as if she had placed a stone upon her shoulders not knowing how to take it off. An ache started at the base of her spine and slowly crawled up her back. She rubbed her shoulders trying to ease the tension that was building there. Aoife thought that she understood the weight her father had to carry now, and for all those years he did it alone. She was grateful to have Liam by her side as they figured out how to best help their kingdom, their people.

The fire crackled as she stroked it to life, trying to warm up the room. The gold from the fire clashed with the silver of the moon streaming in from the window. A calm breeze rustled through the trees shaking them.

Aoife walked to the window shutting it to trap the heat in the room. The winter was much fiercer in Laoch than Saibhreas.

She rolled down her sheets and moved to her dresser by the bed. Pulling off her gown and tucking it away.

A chill gripped her skin causing her to draw closer to the fire. She carefully lowered herself to the hearth getting as close to the fire as she could. She brushed her fingers through the pale golden strands brushing loose her braid.

She shook her head and patted her bulging stomach. She laughed at the awkwardness of her body which refused to get comfortable. The easy part was getting down, how would she get back up? She thought to herself.

The door opened noisily as Liam entered the room. Her heart fluttered, and her face flushed red, he still made her heart jump.

His black hair fell into his face covering his electric blue eyes. He searched for her in the room, clicking his tongue in mock chastisement at finding her on the floor.

"Aoife why are you on the floor?" He moved closer to her extending his hand.

"I was cold," she laughed and taking his hand, "Liam I think I will need your other hand as well, or we will never have enough leverage to set me upright again."

His eyes sparkled with amusement.

"Aye, right you are love."

He bent over and softly kissed the knuckles of her hand before releasing it and crossing behind her and grabbing her underneath her arms, hauling her to her feet. She turned around to face him as he wrapped his arms around her waist. She brushed back the hair falling into his face to get a better look into his eyes. They softened as she smiled up at him.

"How is the little one doing?" He asked motioning to her stomach.

She shook her head in mock scorn, "She is a bird, fluttering her day away trying to escape."

"You think it's a girl then?" He kissed her forehead.

"Well one can hope." She walked away from his grasp over to the edge of the bed and sat down. He changed into his tunic laying down his sword. He never slept without it by him, a warrior's habit.

"I have some news love." Liam smiled at her mischief lighting up his eyes. "Oh, is it good news?"

"Well I think so but perhaps you will have another opinion."

"Tell me Liam, what is it?"

"I have asked Malcolm and Maeve to come stay here for a while."

"WHAT?!" She yelled and jumped to her feet. "You aren't teasing me, are you? Oh Liam, truthfully!!" She went over to him and wrapped her arms around his neck. "Why are they coming back? Is anything wrong?"

"Well they are making good progress, but I have heard word that Maeve made a promise to my queen to be here for the birth of our baby. And I will not be the one responsible for that promise not being kept. Malcolm also sent news that she too is with child."

Aoife started to laugh and cry all at once.

Maeve was also with child? Life was too kind. When the energy was spent all she felt was pure joy. He kissed her soundly on the mouth pressing her body closer to him engulfing her body in his arms.

The door swung open suddenly as two little boys ran into the room. Swords in their hands. One had the coloring of night. The other of day.

Her boys, Cahal and Eamonn were born the same day, Cahal had eyes like his father blue as a summer day and hair like sunshine, and he was a serious one. The other, Caelan was taller and broader had hair dark as night and his eyes were the color of iron, the color of her father's eyes, an easy smile was usually found on his face.

"What's wrong mam?" they frantically looked around the room.

Pride etched in their faces and shoulders.

"Your mam received good news and she can be quite loud when she is happy." Liam teased.

Aoife swatted at her husband bringing a chuckle from him as her sons lowered their swords, their muscles uncoiling. Her boys were born to be warriors taking after their father.

"Aunt Maeve is coming soon. Now go back to bed now we have an early start in the morning if you are to go with your father to the village." They looked at each other and turned to their parents.

"Can we have a story? Just one! Please!" They pleaded.

Aoife smiled and nodded toward the bed "Alright but just one because you were my brave warriors coming to my aid."

All three of her men surrounded her on the bed.

"Have I ever told you the story of the princess who fought alongside a wolf prince?" Liam slipped his hand into hers, laughter lighting up his features.

Their eyes serious as they shook their heads back and forth.

"Well my boys it all began when the princess traveled through the woods."

The End

Acknowledgements

Thanks to those who believed in this book and me: Karly, Patricija, Maisie, Dallin, Maja, Blair, Kimber, Maria. It takes a village to make a book. I want to thank my parents for instilling in me a love of reading. And to my grandmas Alice and Kerry and my grandpa Randy for always supporting me in anything I do. Thank you to my siblings Kelli, Kenzie and Boden for always keeping it real.

87479111R00139

Made in the USA
San Bernardino, CA
04 September 2018